Heart Trouble

TOMMIE CONRAD

CRIMSON
ROMANCE

F+W Media, Inc.

This edition published by
Crimson Romance
an imprint of F+W Media, Inc.
10151 Carver Road, Suite 200
Blue Ash, Ohio 45242
www.crimsonromance.com

To my parents, who made my life possible.

Chapter One

That damned rooster was crowing again.

Brandt Conner pulled the pillow over his head and tried, in vain, to catch another five minutes' worth of winks. When the rooster sang again, he cursed, slid the pillow aside, and glanced at the clock. Day was breaking outside, and his father would already be at the kitchen table poring over the newspaper and sipping his morning coffee. Brandt struggled from the warm blankets and, naked save for his underwear, plodded toward the closet. He pulled on the first pair of jeans he found—they were neatly folded so he figured they were clean—and quickly buttoned a flannel shirt across his chest. Socks and Western work boots completed the ensemble. In the bathroom, he did his business, finger-combed his hair, and yawned all the way down the stairs.

It was never quiet in the old ranch house. The stairs squeaked, the ancient nails shifting in and out of the risers with each footstep. The walls settled and groaned at all hours of the day. The place was well-insulated behind the lath and plaster—it'd been blown in just two years earlier—but nothing could stop the march of time, the floors sloping here and there as the stone foundation settled beneath antique floor joists. Brandt knew it'd take a gut job to fix all that was wrong with the place, but his father insisted the house had great bones and would outlast them all. A noncommittal "maybe" was the only answer Brandt could ever muster in most situations.

Mitchell Conner sat in his regular chair at the kitchen table, the one he'd repaired with nails and wood glue more than a few times.

It squeaked and groaned like everything else in the house. He shared his son's brown hair, though it'd gone grey at the temples a long time ago, matching his weathered face. He sipped from his coffee cup—he drank it black, stout enough to walk on its own, never adding milk or sugar. Brandt had tried that once, and found out quickly that he'd rather drink tar or crude oil than to ever again try coffee without milk.

"Good afternoon," Mitchell joked. Brandt considered a rancorous comeback for a moment before he reconsidered. It was just his father's way, he knew—he'd been trying for twenty-five years to turn his only child into an upright man, and maybe he'd succeeded. Brandt still lived at home and helped take care of the ranch, despite his college degree. The degree was superfluous, however, because Brandt had never wanted to be anything but a cattle rancher. Being a cowboy was as easy as breathing; being a dutiful son was more difficult. Brandt took a seat at the table, and kept his thoughts to himself. His mother, Laura, was a tad gentler, a more sympathetic counterpoint to her gruff husband.

"Good morning, sweetheart," she said, her back turned to him. She stood over the range, the newest appliance in the house, and plated breakfast for him. She rested a hand lightly on his shoulder as she set eggs, toast, and bacon before him, joining it a moment later with a glass of milk.

"Thanks, Mom," Brandt said before he picked up his fork and dug in. This was usually the calmest, most serene part of his day: dishes clinking together, the rustling of the newsprint as his father flipped through it. His father read the paper deliberately, quietly, and Brandt could never remember him voicing an opinion over its contents. He and Laura made small talk as she ate her own breakfast, and that was that.

"Brandt." Mitchell folded the paper closed and father and son locked eyes.

"Yeah, Dad?"

"Don't forget I need you to head into town this morning and pick up that new roll of fence at the farm store."

Brandt chewed for half a minute before he answered. "You don't need me to check the herd this morning?"

Mitchell shook his head quickly. "I'll get Rawlings to help me with that. Besides, you need a better rapport with people. Most everyone finds you a little…" Brandt's mouth dropped in a frown at one corner. "Broody."

Brandt lifted an eyebrow. "Okay. As soon as I'm done eating, I'll head into Layton." He cleared his throat. "Is it on your tab or…"

Mitchell pulled a wad of cash from his pocket and passed it across the table—five twenty-dollar bills. "That oughta cover it." He shoved his chair back, its legs scraping the pine boards, and stood. "Drive safe, son." He pulled his hat from a hook near the back door and left without another word.

"He's not trying to be harsh," Laura insisted, and Brandt knew it was to his benefit to listen. "He's just from a different generation. Warmth is not his strong suit."

Brandt nodded and finished his breakfast. "I know," he replied, shoving the bills in his jeans. He stood, grabbed his cowboy hat, and nearly had it slung atop his head before he remembered to give his mother a kiss on the cheek. "Later, Mom. Don't work too hard today."

She smiled up at him warmly, both hands locked around her own cup of coffee. "I'll try not to, sweetie."

The Conner ranch covered not quite forty-five acres on the outskirts of Layton, a town where everyone was a farmer, a future farmer, or a farmer's daughter. This was the section of Kentucky that featured gently rolling meadows, a safe respite from the rocky foothills and limestone canyons that dotted points north and east, the verdant pastures and meadows providing ample land for cattle grazing. Other farms featured a passel of hogs, goats, even sheep, but the Conners never cottoned to anything but beef cattle and poultry. And that was just fine with Brandt—cattle were enough work, and he'd been dragging pails of milk and baskets of eggs in the house since he was big enough to walk. It was a lifestyle that both his parents were born into, and complaining about it wouldn't have done much good—he had an advantage on both of them, having been indoctrinated in the importance of a college education by his parents from an early age. He'd read Shakespeare, researched in that big library until his eyes had gone crossed, learned all about the difference between the philosophies of Aristotle and Plato, and earned that four-year degree. There were times, when he was alone with his thoughts, that he couldn't understand why all of it was so important—it wasn't like he'd ever had to recite a sonnet down at the farm store. You asked for feed, or fence wire, or iodine. You paid the clerk or had it put on your father's tab. Not exactly rocket science.

There was some advantage to being an only child, and primary beneficiary of his parents' affections. If Mitchell was somewhat gruff and distant, Brandt had never wanted for anything. His closet was full of flannels and jeans, and he had plenty of nice boots and warm coats. Good gloves that kept his hands from getting raw and chapped in the winter. A few nice Stetson hats. A black truck that was in his name and still under warranty. His dad paid only the insurance, and upkeep otherwise fell on his shoulders. As hard as ranch life could be from time to time, Brandt figured he was luckier than most—how many kids got to live out a childhood dream every day of their adult lives?

It was early spring, the world outside the truck windows greening back to life. The redbuds were still colored with their bright blooms, the green leaves a few days away from bursting forth. Brandt cracked his window long enough to get a taste of the chilled air, then powered it back up and into place. It was a few miles into Layton, and this was the biggest stretch of quiet he ever got to experience. There was no silence to be found on the ranch, whether in or out of the house. There was always something more to do, something else to worry over, someone yelling for you to get your muddy damned boots off the back porch …

Here in the truck, though, he heard nothing but the hum of the engine and his subtle breathing. He rolled on toward town, past the high school with its brand-new bleachers and running track paved in broken asphalt. In his years there, he'd consistently baffled the track coach, who couldn't figure out why someone with a sprinter's legs didn't try out for the team. Brandt had always shrugged it off; he'd outrun a few bulls in his time, mainly because he didn't listen to his father's carefully-worded warnings not to piss them off. No matter—he'd never been injured on the ranch, aside from Mitchell reaming him up one side and down the other. Laura always defused conflict before it reached critical mass, a better peacemaker than anyone at the Ambassador's table.

Brandt had always been closer to his mother, from the time he was born. Mitchell had taught him everything there was to know about ranching, how to brand a cow or inoculate a calf, even how to turn a bull into a steer, but so much of that was technical, distant, as though the elder Conner was keeping his son at arm's length. "Do this, not that. Stand up straight, don't pout." And so it went. Maybe that was the real reason he'd been marched off to college, he considered, pulling his truck into a diagonal space at the front of the farm store.

To keep him and his father from coming to blows.

• • •

Different day, same routine.

In the week since Marissa Sloan had started her job at Layton Farm and Supply Company, she'd done the same tasks each day: swept the floor every morning before they opened for business, but not before she'd inventoried and straightened all the shelves, wiped down the checkout counter, and started the coffee in the employee lounge that was little more than a cubbyhole between the restroom and storeroom. The manager, Mona Larkin, was a longtime friend of her mother who'd secured this job for her. The only stipulation was that she had to move from her hometown, not quite fifty miles away, which was no hardship—she had nothing holding her there, and thus far her college degree had proven useless. She was now renting the apartment above the farm store, the one that always smelled like seasoned lumber and feed corn. As she put away the broom, she gave the store a once-over— the interior was covered in aged wood, and looked like it would turn into a tinderbox if she breathed on it too warmly. Mona had given her a customary greeting as she unlocked the front door before heading back into the sanctuary of her office. Mona would never have made manager without a strong degree of nepotism— she didn't display a whole lot of friendliness outside of superficial greetings: "Hi, how are you?" or "How is your (insert family member's name here)?" was about as deep as she ever went. Still, Marissa was exceedingly grateful for this job, and the opportunity to earn a paycheck. She'd been without both for too long.

She was settling in for another standard day, her butt planted firmly on a stool beside the cash register, when her world was knocked sideways. He ambled into the store, coughing as dust motes filled the air, a hitch barely noticeable in his gait. The white Stetson was pushed low, shielding his eyes from view. As he stepped close to the counter, she looked up into his gaze.

Her eyes swept over a wiry, rangy frame, his jeans and shirt well broken-in. He pushed up the brim of his hat and she caught her first glimpse of those green eyes—darker than an oak leaf, closer in hue to a blade of grass. His face was lightly tanned, nearly blending in with his brown hair. He had a sharp jawline but little else to distinguish an otherwise handsome face. When their gazes met, the back of her neck went hot, and she was suddenly relieved she'd worn her hair down that day. He cleared his throat and gave her a small smile.

"Good morning," he said in a roughened timbre.

"Good morning," she replied.

"I'm here to pick up an order," he murmured.

"Okay," she said, a little taken aback by his abruptness. She rifled in her pocket until she found the key that opened the storage locker under the counter, the usual place where special orders were housed.

"Haven't seen you around here before," he continued, and she noted he'd shoved his hands in his pockets. Don't look at his pockets, she chided herself. Don't look anywhere but his eyes—beautiful, green, mysterious.

"I just started this week..." she said, trailing off as Mona entered the corner of her vision. She'd undoubtedly heard the whoosh of air when their first customer arrived for the day and come to supervise. Marissa reminded herself once more that she needed this job and would slowly have to earn Mona's respect.

"Brandt," Mona said, somewhat tersely.

"Mrs. Larkin," he replied.

"I noticed your mama wasn't in church Sunday. I hope she's feeling okay."

He nodded politely, but Marissa noted the square set of his jaw, as though speaking required great effort for him. "She was feeling a little under the weather. She's fine now."

"Good," Mona replied. Marissa set the bundle of electric fence atop the counter and Mona shot her a mildly exasperated look. "Don't forget the insulators, Marissa. They should be right alongside the fencing."

Marissa found the bag of yellow plastic insulators immediately and laid them next to the fence. She was perceptive enough to notice the uncomfortable pose displayed by manager and customer, standing far apart on the other side of the counter, as though a chasm had opened between them. She wondered what that was all about, and then realized it was none of her business.

"Brandt," Mona said in a measured tone, "this is Marissa Sloan. She just started working for us." He extended his hand across the counter and she shook it. His handshake was firm, the skin warm and work-hewn.

"Nice to meet you," he said.

"Likewise," she replied. She noted quickly that he couldn't speak to anyone without meeting their eyes. Eye contact wasn't her strong suit but this cowboy or whatever he was had her seemingly hypnotized. Their hands parted and he looked down at his purchases before meeting her eyes again.

"How much do I owe you?" She totaled the items, told him the price, and money and change was traded.

"Do you need a receipt?"

He nodded. "Tax purposes. You understand."

"Of course," she said, playing along. She dropped the receipt in his bag and he started to go. "Have a nice day," she quickly remembered to say.

He gave her an appraising look, then spared another smile. "You too, ma'am," he said, touching the brim of his hat. She watched him the whole way, only breaking her stare when he disappeared and the door closed behind him. She felt the blush creep along her neck again, her insides turning molten. She met Mona's eyes—she swore they were black, a totally unnatural color for anyone's irises—and found them staring back at her hard.

"Who was that?" Marissa asked, trying to keep her tone nonchalant and disinterested.

Mona frowned. "Brandt Conner. His family owns a big cattle ranch outside of town."

"Cattle ranch?" She gave her boss a quizzical stare. "I thought people called them farms around here."

She shook her head. "Most do, but I guess the Conners have a better PR agent." She laughed under her breath. "Most farms have a variety of animals, but the Conners only deal in cattle. And they keep a few chickens around for eggs."

Marissa stared at her fingers as she began tapping them on the plastic covering that formed the top of the counter. "He seemed friendly."

"Oh, he is," Mona retorted. Their eyes met again, and Marissa didn't like what she saw there.

"You said his name was Brandt?"

Mona nodded. "You'd be wise to wipe that interested look off your face, young lady. Brandt is a first-class player. His parents might just as well install a turnstile at the top of their stairs. He's already left a trail of broken hearts from there to here," she said, sweeping her hand from the front of the store to the back. "If you're looking for love, come to church with me this week. There are plenty of well-spoken, God-fearing men there who are looking for long-term commitment. With Brandt Conner, commitment lasts about as long as it takes to get his pants off."

"I'll try to remember that, Mona," Marissa replied quietly, anxious for the woman to be out of her hair and no longer spouting gibberish. She'd literally gazed upon Brandt for the first time five minutes ago—and while she was undoubtedly attracted, she hardly needed Mona to dissuade her from anything. She was old enough at twenty-four to make her own decisions, to form her own view of the world. Her own father had shown her that male reliability was not a given, and her luck with past boyfriends had been mixed. But this was a new town, a fresh start, and Mona was the only person here she knew. As her manager walked back to the safety of her office, Marissa couldn't help but think she'd like to add Brandt to her short list of friends. With Mona's door shut tight, she pulled a ledger from beneath the counter and scanned its alphabetical listings. The Conners had a standing account, and looked to be frequent customers. With any luck, she'd see Brandt again soon.

Time would tell.

Chapter Two

Brandt turned the radio up on his drive home, beleaguered from that one short trip to the farm store. Nothing like a visit with Mona to turn a man's entire day to shit in a hurry. He rolled his eyes and kept his focus on the road ahead. He'd be home soon enough, listening to cows bellow. Listening to his father bellow. "God," he said aloud. "Sometimes I'd just like to run away from it all and never come back." No matter how much he loved the ranch, there were days that he thought his head might explode. He turned under the ranch sign and pulled up into the driveway, and found his father standing near the barn with Brandt's best friend, Rawlings McCoy.

Brandt couldn't remember a time when he and Rawlings weren't friends—the origin went back further than either of them could recollect, and Rawlings had pretty much grown up on the Conner Ranch. Without indicting the McCoys too harshly, Brandt knew that Mitchell and Laura had done a better job of rearing Rawlings than his own parents had. The McCoys had just had too damned many kids, with middle-child Rawlings falling through the cracks but always finding a safe haven at the Conner home. He might just as well have been Brandt's brother—he had a lighter shade of brown hair, brown eyes, and they were about the same height. If Rawlings wore a tall enough boot, they could see eye-to-eye. Upon reaching his eighteenth birthday, Rawlings had left home and moved to a small bunkhouse on the ranch and set about learning everything there was to know about beef cattle. He considered that his form of higher education. Brandt had been away at college, and in some ways Rawlings had been the stand-in son, though it had long been clear that Mitchell and Laura loved him not as a surrogate child but as if he was their own. Brandt couldn't imagine loving that guy more if they were blood kin. Not that men ever talked about love in such a manner. It was enough knowing that he and Rawlings always had each other's backs.

Rawlings lifted a hand to wave at him as he pulled his truck into park and rolled down the window. Mitchell was, as usual, more subdued.

"I want you two to get that fence completed today," Mitchell reminded them. "We don't need any escapees this year." Brandt recalled how they'd spent the better part of two days last year, in the hottest part of summer, trying to round up two stray calves than had gone in search of a fresher pond. He went off milk for a week after that one, the very sight of it turning his stomach.

"Yes, sir," Rawlings replied.

"Yeah, Dad," Brandt said in his usual monotone. "We'll get right on it." Rawlings was sliding into his truck just as quickly as he engaged the door lock, and Brandt pulled into drive without sparing his father another glance. They were headed across the ranch, but his mind remained firmly on Marissa.

"I shut off the breaker." Rawlings pointed out, clearly eager to start conversation. "Mitch told me not to forget and I didn't."

"Good man," Brandt replied.

"What's wrong?"

"Hmm?"

"You and your dad. There's enough tension between the two of you to pull a four-wheeler out of the mud."

"Same old, same old," he murmured. "Dad always seems to think I lack initiative or I'm just too damned lazy to care. He doesn't consider that I might just be a quiet sort of fellow."

"Uh-huh," Rawlings teased, adjusting his black hat. "So how was Layton this morning?"

"Uneventful." Brandt bobbed his wrist atop the steering wheel. He could practically drive this section of pasture blindfolded, and with one finger. It was smooth, free of obstructions, one of the herd's favorite grazing spots. "They've got a new girl working down at the farm store."

Rawlings's already bright face lifted even more. "What's she look like, man?"

Brandt tried to remember her in his mind's eye: long, straight blonde hair, halfway down her back, not fixed any special way. Cute nose, cute mouth, nice, round face. Blue eyes, maybe? He couldn't recall. Sweet voice. Breasts straining against her shirt. Skin that he was already eager to taste. "She was freakin' hot, man. She looked good."

"When was the last time you got laid?" Rawlings asked without preamble. Brandt nearly choked on his own saliva. He did a few mental calculations before answering.

"It's been a while," he surmised. "What about you?"

Rawlings laughed. "Um, what year is it?" Brandt gave him a quick glance and their eyes met. "Exactly. It's been that long."

Brandt shook his head. "Dry spell for both of us."

"What about Dee Wilson?" Rawlings asked, recovering quickly from his embarrassment.

Brandt chuckled hoarsely. "A part of me wanted her. You know which part. Luckily my brain said no, and that's what I listened to." He shook his head again. "Do you know how many men she's tried to rope into engagements by saying, 'Oops, I'm pregnant'? And then it turns out there's never a baby. I didn't trust her not to poke holes in the condom."

"Speaking of women, did you see Mona?"

Brandt groaned. "Unfortunately." The truck hit a bump and they both bounced against the seatbelts. "She still hasn't gotten over it."

"She thinks you broke her daughter's heart."

He laughed ruefully. "I may have been dating Britt Larkin, but I wasn't the only man she was seeing. You know what I mean."

Rawlings snorted. "You ain't gotta paint me a picture, Conner. I guess what Mama don't know won't hurt her."

"Maybe." Brandt parked along the edge of the ranch and shut down his engine. "I don't know where this reputation came from that I'm some kind of hound dog. All I ask for is monogamy in a relationship. Even if I know it's never going amount to nothing more than good sex, I'm still a one-woman man."

"Hell," Rawlings said. "I'd settle for just the good sex at this point."

Brandt smiled. "You've gotta get off this ranch a little more often, pal. Get out into town, see what's happening in the real world."

"Like you, loverboy? Flirting at the farm store?" Brandt grinned and gathered up his supplies. Rawlings already had the pliers in his coat and was itching to work.

"Maybe," he said.

"So what's this mystery girl's name?"

Brandt closed the door behind him and checked the old wire. It wasn't hot, so he and Rawlings set to work removing it and the worn insulators from atop the metal stakes.

"I think it was Marissa. Mona introduced us, albeit reluctantly. Like I was radioactive sludge all young women should avoid."

Rawlings removed the insulators while he coiled the wire, brittle and rusted in places. "Maybe you oughta tell her the truth."

Brandt was careful not to unleash a huge laugh at that one. "Mrs. Larkin, I hate to break it to you, but your twenty-five year-old daughter isn't a virgin. In fact, she's had more bedmates than the average young man of her age." He smirked at his best friend. "That'd go over like a lead balloon."

"Good point."

"Besides," he continued, "unless you're like my parents and marry the only person you've ever dated, it's hard to get through life without breaking someone's heart. I didn't like the way things went down between us but you don't see me running around town besmirching her good name."

"That's because you, Mr. Conner, are a gentleman," Rawlings said in a good-natured, albeit affected, tone. They walked slowly with the new coil of fencing, unspooling it and securing it with insulators as they went. Rawlings held the coil as Brandt hammered each section into place. "Had you ever seen this Marissa before?"

Brandt shook his head. "Uh-uh. Must not be from around here or we'd have seen her in school at some point. She's probably about our age, if I had to guess."

"Blonde, brunette, or redhead?"

"Blonde—natural too."

"Nice."

"I don't know, Rawlings," he said, pausing to stare at a copse of trees. "It feels kind of like…"

"Like what?" he asked with carefully veiled impatience.

"Like I just got hit by a bolt of lightning."

When they worked together, and on a fairly basic task, they generally finished with time to spare. Still, they inspected each yard of fence carefully—Rawlings, eager to impress his boss, and Brandt, less than eager to hear from his father that he'd missed something. Brandt found that there was something of a burden to being an only child—true, he didn't have to fight a sibling for a place in the ranch, but he also couldn't make one misstep without it being viewed a catastrophe. Laura had told him once or twice that they'd tried for other children, but it just wasn't meant to be. She was happy to have one perfect child, while Brandt figured Mitchell had resigned himself to the prospect many years earlier. Sometimes Brandt felt sorry for his father—and other times, he just felt sorry for himself. Then again, he thought, there was

Rawlings—big family and no place to fit in. Thank God they were friends. Thank God Rawlings was the buffer he needed, the one Mitchell never had to criticize.

"You wanna come over to my place for lunch?" Rawlings asked excitedly. They were climbing back in the cab now, and Brandt slung the old, rusted wire in the bed of his truck.

"What you got?" he asked with a smile.

"Chili in the crockpot. Made it myself," Rawlings said proudly.

His smile was contagious, and before he knew it, Brandt was grinning like a fool. "Sure," he answered. "I'd love to."

• • •

"I saw my brother this weekend."

Brandt had been glancing around the bunkhouse, the place every inch a bachelor pad. The entertainment center had been constructed from concrete blocks and two-by-fours, and was as sturdy as anything from a furniture showroom. The couch and chairs were mismatched. Even the dining table was a cast-off from the Conner home, now down to two spindly chairs. The nicest thing in the whole place was the television—and maybe the crockpot.

"He's married, right?" Brandt asked to fill dead space in the air. He knew Rawlings wasn't close to his brother or three sisters—or was it four?—so he didn't press the issue.

Rawlings handed him a steaming bowl, the room now redolent with the scents of tomatoes, chili powder, and saltine crackers. They both dove into their lunch without hesitancy. "Yeah," he answered around a mouthful of hamburger and beans. "They just had a baby boy."

Brandt nodded. "Saw that in the paper."

"Uh-huh." He swallowed, then grimaced a bit. "He said Dad didn't even drop by the hospital."

Brandt noted the sadness behind his friend's eyes, the carefully-crafted exterior. On the outside, Rawlings was stainless steel. On the inside, he craved love as much as anyone. "That sucks." He swallowed and cleared his throat. "They're happy though, right? Brady and his wife?"

"Yeah," he replied, his face lifting. "Pretty rare and special thing, that, when you look at where we came from."

"You're happy," Brandt prodded. "Huh? Huh?" He grinned until Rawlings joined him.

"I guess," he said with a quick laugh. "I have a great job and a pretty good life. Mitch treats me like I'm blood."

"You'll always be welcome around here," Brandt said, cocking his head to one side for emphasis. "Though someday, I figure one of us is gonna get married and move off the place."

"Shit, no," Rawlings protested. "Remember when we were kids, and we *swore* we'd never get married?"

Brandt nodded. He finished his chili and laughed. "We also swore we'd never kiss a girl. I guess that's a promise both of us have broken."

"More than once," Rawlings agreed. He stood and carted the two bowls to the sink. "Hey, maybe this Marissa girl will have a friend, and we could double date."

Brandt laughed some more. "I just met the girl, I'm pretty sure she doesn't even know my last name, but you're creating a relationship for me *and* you. Smooth, guy, smooth."

Rawlings leaned back against the counter, crossing one booted ankle over the other. "They always did say I was a crafty devil, Brandt."

"And they were right," Brandt agreed, his mouth broadening into a huge smile as he simply shook his head.

•••

Marissa had survived another day. She hung up her sales clerk tag for the evening.

Mona had given her first the stink-eye and then the cold shoulder, presumably for daring to even smile and then show interest in Brandt. What was she supposed to do—ignore the cowboy whom she didn't know from Adam based on a snippet of small-town gossip? That didn't constitute good customer service, and coming from her background, she knew better than to take another's jaundiced word seriously.

As a small-town girl herself, the progeny of an absentee father and a mother who meant well but often stumbled along life's journey, Marissa was well-versed in the power of slings and arrows, barbs others cast without realizing she was within earshot. Oh, they'd always apologize: "I didn't mean anything by it, dear," but only because they'd been caught. She'd never gone hungry—her mother had worked to ensure that Marissa always had the essentials—so what right did anyone have to put her down? If she never saw Brandt again or he dropped by every day with a cup of coffee, it was certainly none of Mona's business.

"I'm overly defensive," Marissa whispered to herself, "and great at creating fantasy relationships inside my own head." Which was true, to a degree. She had no actual memories of her father, only old photos. He'd left before she'd developed an awareness of him, even a sensory memory. Some fathers smelled like tobacco or sawdust or peppermint, but her father just smelled absent. She imagined, often, what he looked like now, how he must be aging, his sandy blonde hair turning platinum with age. To her knowledge he'd never remarried or had other children, but she also lacked even basic knowledge aside from his address, inked in on yearly correspondence. He sent her a birthday card, like clockwork, arriving in the correct week each year. And that was it—he sent a check, so he must have a job, some livelihood that occupied his days. Marissa wished, perhaps foolishly, that she might occupy his thoughts, if he ever wondered how she was, not as the product of a short-lived marriage but as his progeny, a flesh-and-blood thing with hopes and dreams and fears and petty annoyances. Maybe she'd never find out.

She was at the supermarket now, muttering to herself as she examined canned foods. She'd never really developed a taste for any particular cuisine. She would eat pretty much anything her mother cooked, and was glad to have it, just the two of them eating quietly in their yellow kitchen. If her mother had been pissed or disappointed at being left to raise her daughter alone, she never let it show. She'd worked to get Marissa the best life and education possible, even as the worry lines formed along her eyes and mouth year after year. Or perhaps Marissa was wrong, and her mother cried alone in her room at night, her hands aching after another eight-hour shift at the cardboard box plant.

Marissa felt a sudden pang of guilt at moving to Layton, even though her mother had encouraged it, finagled the job for her. How lonely she must be, with Marissa miles away, in another state. She resolved then to call her that night, even if the minutiae of her day were pretty boring. She had kind of met a hot cowboy. That was worth sharing.

She was switching a box of spaghetti in her cart for a box of penne when a familiar shock of red hair caught her eye. No, it couldn't be. "Rowan?"

A tall woman with curly red hair turned around, her face of surprise turning quickly into a smile. "Marissa Sloan, how in the hell are you?" They exchanged a quick hug. Marissa and Rowan had never been that tight in high school, but they'd been casual friends, sharing a lot of the same classes and even a few group projects.

"I'm good," she replied, still a little bewildered. "How…"

"How did I wind up in Layton?" she guessed. She moved her shopping cart out of the middle of the aisle, where she'd been tying up traffic. Marissa nodded. "I moved here last year, took a teaching job at the high school. It's been pretty good, actually. The kids here are curious and willing to learn, or at least more so than the ones from my student teaching days. It's been refreshing, to say the least."

"I just moved here last week," Marissa replied. "It seems like a nice place to live."

"Do you know anyone around here?" Rowan inquired. "I've mainly just met colleagues at school."

"A few people," Marissa said. "Mainly the Larkins, who own the farm store. My mom knows the manager, Mona, from way back. And after two years of unemployment, I was ready for the first thing that came along."

Rowan frowned. "I hear that. You finished college, right?"

Marissa nodded. "I spent hours working on graduate school applications and essays, burned through entire weekends focused on nothing but. I had all these ideas and plans about how I wanted to parlay my degree into something therapeutic. Joke was on me, I guess. No graduate school wanted me, nor did any employer."

"That really sucks," Rowan answered. Marissa could see the genuine empathy and concern emitting from her green eyes. "I'll keep my ears open for any job openings in the school system." She glanced around quickly, checking for eavesdroppers or anyone within earshot. It wasn't a large store. "Just between you and me, if you'd be willing to complete the requirements, you'd make a far better guidance counselor than those hacks at school."

Marissa laughed. "We had those in our day too, didn't we?"

"Uh-huh."

"Anyway, I'd appreciate that." Marissa looked in her cart, noticed that she was buying pasta but no sauce, cereal but no milk. She really was a space cadet. "Look, I should give you my phone number. That way I can say I have at least one friend in town."

Rowan opened her purse and began to jot down her contact information. "Are you married yet?"

"No," Marissa replied softly. "Honestly, my parents' divorce has always made me gun-shy about long-term commitment."

"I understand." Rowan handed her a slip of paper and Marissa did the same. "I'm still in the hunt for love myself. And all the male teachers at the high school are married. Oops. Keep an eye out for a good-looking man, and I'll do the same. Agreed?"

Marissa laughed, her mouth forming into a small smile. Maybe it was joy at seeing an old friend in an unfamiliar place. Or it may have had something to do with the faint image of Brandt that flickered across her subconscious. Either way, she didn't smile much these days, and it felt good. "Agreed."

Chapter Three

Brandt clawed his way out of bed a little easier the next morning, maybe because he awoke due to some internal mechanism rather than the rooster's crow. Sometimes he slept hard enough that not even a crash of lightning could stir him, the kind that hit too hard, flashed too bright and hot across the sky, with an intensity that should've signaled the end of the world. Even rain pounding hard on the tin roof, sounding like it would drown them all in their beds, couldn't rouse him. Two things worked every time, though—his father's voice and his father's fist on the door. Those never failed.

He yawned the whole way down the stairs, and scratched at some invisible itch beneath his shirt. He found only his mother at the breakfast table, sipping coffee and reading a paperback novel. "There's a plate warming for you in the oven, Brandt," Laura announced. He nodded even though their eyes never met, retrieved his food, and poured a glass of milk before taking his usual seat at the table. It may have been childish but he always, always put his scrambled eggs and sausage between the two slices of toast and ate them as a sandwich. He was half done before he bothered to ask the question hanging on the end of his tongue.

"Mom, where is Dad?"

Laura smiled at him. "Out in the barn with Rawlings, checking on a pregnant cow."

Brandt was aware of the heifer; while they dealt primarily in beef, they bred a cow or two as needed in order to keep the milk flowing. "Do I need to get out there? Did he say anything to you about it?"

"Not today, Brandt. I actually have an errand for you to run."

"I'm listening," he said, mouth full of food.

She took in a deep breath, as though she had something of great import to share. "I need you to head down to the farm store for me and pick up some tomato plants. Big Boy if they have them. Try to get two or three varieties, though."

Brandt finished his milk in a few gulps and wiped his mouth with a napkin. "Mom, can I ask you something?"

"Sure, sweetheart."

"Are you trying to keep me and Dad apart?"

Laura placed her bookmark between the pages, laid the book atop the table, and appraised her son with those pale blue eyes. She pushed a lock of hair behind her ear, the strands vacillating from light brown to red to silver. "You and your father are very much alike, Brandt. I used to think I'd never met a more stubborn man on God's green earth than Mitchell Conner. Then lo and behold, I gave birth to his challenger." She smiled warmly, her face the kindest Brandt had ever known. "Maybe I'm speaking out of turn here, but your father and I have been married since we were eighteen years old. I'm sure some part of him thinks you should have settled down already. But in his heart he knows how lucky he is to have you around here, to know that you still care. There's really no logical reason to stick around a farm or ranch these days, unless you have a passion for it."

Brandt swallowed hard. "That's not the only reason, Mom." He cleared his throat. "It's the right thing to do."

Laura nodded, seeming to understand her son's conviction. In truth, Brandt would have taken any opportunity to get back in town, see Marissa again. Girl had already gotten under his skin, and he'd known her for all of twenty-four hours. He'd wiped down his Stetson last night just in case there was any dirt on it. The boy had it bad, but he certainly wouldn't tell his mother that. He slipped the cash in his wallet, gave her a kiss, and grabbed his hat as he headed out the door. He didn't even bother with the barn—he headed straight for his truck, snapped his seatbelt together, and hit the ground running toward town.

• • •

Two days, two sightings—what were the odds?

Marissa was stocking shelves with her coworker, Josie, when Brandt strode through the door, looking a little like a lost puppy dog. Maybe it was the set of his lips, his mouth open as though he was midsentence and the words suddenly failed him. Or maybe it was the burst of sunlight that outlined his body through the plate-glass windows, giving him this strange, supernatural aura, like he didn't belong on this planet.

Oh, the tricks your eyes can play, Marissa thought to herself.

Brandt was the first to speak. "Do y'all have any tomato plants in yet?"

Marissa nodded, hoping he was addressing her. He must've been talking to her—that's where both eyes were locked, two green circles getting a bead on her face. "Around the side, behind the chicken wire."

He spared a grin. "Do you have time to help me pick out a few? They're for my mom, and I could use a woman's touch."

Marissa glanced around to her compatriot. "Josie, can you cover the register while I help out this customer?"

"Of course," she replied good-naturedly, a smile forming on her lips as she stepped behind the counter.

Marissa nodded her head and Brandt fell into step with her. She felt the whoosh of air that must've come from a hand that had almost been placed to the small of her back before he thought better of it. From the corner of her eye, she noted that both hands were at his sides.

The flowers and vegetables were kept under a shed roof and surrounded on three sides by chicken wire—it wasn't quite a garden center, but too primitive to constitute a greenhouse. It was a setup that seemed to work for both the store and its customers.

The tomatoes had been freshly watered and humidity now hung in the air around them as the droplets began to evaporate. It was a warmer than average spring day, birds providing ample background noise. She let him look around for a moment before she drew close again, catching a whiff of aftershave. It was almost imperceptible, as though he'd just slapped on a drop before reconsidering. He seemed tall standing there, hands on hips—at least six feet, maybe more, and the boots only added to his height.

"You're staring at me," he said, his eyes still trained on the tomato plants. His voice totally disarmed her, made her forget her purpose. Saleslady. That's what she was—the person in charge of making the store money at this moment.

"You said your name was Brandt, right?" A pointless question, uttered in a nervous voice, but it was the best she could do. "And I wasn't staring," she fibbed. He stood in profile, silent and still, and a grin emerged on the corner of his mouth.

"Sounds made up, huh?" He shrugged. "I used to joke with people than my parents couldn't decide between 'Brandon' and 'Barrett' for a first name, so they split the difference." He scraped his boot against the asphalt for a moment. "Truth is, it's my mom's maiden name."

"What's your middle name?" she asked out of sheer curiosity.

"Mitchell, after my dad." His voice turned gravelly at the end, as though his father was a sore subject. She knew something about that.

"Brandt Mitchell Conner. Definitely sounds like a cowboy name."

He laughed somewhere deep in his throat, a purely masculine sound. "Lucky me, growing up into a cowboy, huh?"

"I guess so." She coughed nervously, unnecessarily. "So, tomatoes?"

He turned to face her, the tanned skin of his neck pulsing as he swallowed hard. "Yeah, tomatoes." His smile was friendly, the kind that could make a person jabber on endlessly. And at that moment, Marissa found herself at a loss for words.

"Most folks like Big Boy, or Beefsteak," she began. "Those are popular varieties."

He nodded gently, his face shadowed in the brim of his hat. "My mom mentioned Big Boy by name, so we'll take a few of those. And the Beefsteak too." He glanced around. "You have a cart or something I could put them in?"

She looked below the shelves until her eyes locked on a plastic tray. She handed it to him and he began to fill it himself. "Let me take that for you…"

"No, ma'am," he said, cutting her off. His warm palm rested atop her hand for a split-second as he dismissed her overture. "I've got two strong arms." He hummed to himself. "Any green tomatoes?"

"Yes," she said, pointing them out for his benefit. He reached for those plants too, and their eyes met.

"There's few things better than a fried green tomato," he reasoned. "Except maybe a first kiss."

She watched his back stiffen, the nervousness working its way across his limbs and toward his face. This was crazy, she thought. She'd met Brandt a whole twenty-four hours earlier and she couldn't seem to think of anything else. She could feel a lonesome butterfly knocking around in her stomach, willing her to speak, calling her a fool. The men she'd dated in the past took a little while to crawl into her head, make her lose her train of thought and better judgment. Brandt, on the other hand, showed up out of the blue and caused the logical sector of her brain to shut down completely. If he asked her to crawl in his truck at this very moment, find a more secluded spot where she could yank off his boots, she probably would have said yes.

"I don't know why I said that," he spoke, ducking his head apologetically. "My mind's all over the place these days."

"I know the feeling."

He nodded at that and they both fell into silence. He held the tray full of green, sticky plants between them defensively—one step closer and he'd probably turn and run. When her eyes looked away from his, he said, "Marissa?"

She quickly looked up into his face again. "Yes?"

"Are you…I mean, do you work this weekend?"

"No," she replied softly.

"Are you…seeing anyone? I noticed you're not wearing a ring," he said, nodding his head toward her hand.

"No," she repeated. "I'm single."

"Me too," he said, and for the first time she noticed the sides of his neck redden. Even Brandt, she thought, wasn't immune to such a human reaction. Should she make him squirm? Play hard-to-get? She could hear the sounds of cars driving past, trucks pulling in and out of the store's parking lot. If she lingered out here too much longer, she'd get an earful from Mona.

"Brandt, what are we doing? Chemistry-testing ourselves?"

He laughed nervously, just barely opened his mouth to speak. "I'm trying to find a decent way to ask you out on a date, Marissa." He shifted his feet nervously. "I just don't know how gentlemanly and appropriate it is when you've just met someone."

Marissa softened her stance, tried with deliberateness to appear more receptive to him. "Imagine if this was a blind date, and we'd never met before. Would you walk into a restaurant, see my face, and walk right back out?"

He laughed again, but far more confidently this time. "That's a loaded question if I've ever heard one, Miss Sloan."

"I don't play fair."

"No, not with that smile." He grinned. "Are you free tomorrow night?"

She didn't answer right away, watching him shift forward as though he expected her to whisper the answer in his ear. "I am."

"Where do you live?"

"Upstairs."

His eyes drifted upward. "Convenient."

"Very."

He gave her a probing look. "Pick you up around seven?"

She nodded. "Casual?"

He laughed. "I'll stay me. You stay you. Sound good?"

"Very."

"Good." He expelled a huge burst of air and she couldn't help but smirk. Had he really been standing there, hanging on every word, forgetting to breathe like a normal human being?

Definitely.

"My phone is in my pocket," he said, hitching his chin toward the square of fabric near his heart. "Why don't you put your number in just in case something comes up and I need to reschedule."

She extended a hand, with all the timidity of a child reaching for the classroom door on the first day of kindergarten, her fingers feeling flannel and the faint impression of hard muscle beneath. Their eyes met, his gaze unreadable beneath the brim of his hat, and she tore her eyes away and keyed in her number.

"There you go," she said, slipping the phone back in his pocket. "I'm hoping you won't need to rain check me, though."

He laughed, and gave her a nervous, gentle smile. "Same here."

She held the door open for him, felt the rush of refrigerated air when they stepped back inside. Josie rang up his purchases, he paid, and then Brandt turned to her and mouthed an awkward goodbye. She simply nodded, their eyes connecting as he pushed through the front door with his back.

"Wow," Josie said when the door closed behind him.

Marissa turned to her. "What?"

"He has eyes for you."

She tried to play it cool. "Do you think so? I just met him."

"So?" Josie scoffed playfully. "Haven't you ever heard of 'love at first sight'?"

Marissa frowned. "I don't know—do you believe in all of that?"

"Maybe," she answered with a shrug. "I've seen Brandt Conner plenty of times, and he doesn't do a thing for me, but he sure put the light in your eyes."

"Ha-ha," Marissa replied drily, glancing around the inside of the store. She saw Mona's door open, and leaned conspiratorially toward her co-worker. "Let's keep this between the two of us, okay?"

"Sure," Josie replied with a smile. "We girls have to stick together, don't we?"

Marissa nodded. "Definitely."

•••

Brandt parked his truck alongside the back porch and unloaded the tomato plants there—he figured his mom would inspect them later—and headed straight for the barn. The sun had transformed the cool weather of yesterday into a pleasingly warm spring day, and had put an extra spring in his step. Or maybe that was the fact that he'd just picked up a date at the farm store. It wasn't his usual pick-up spot, but then again, nothing about Marissa struck him as usual. That sort of assessing look she'd given him there in front of the tomatoes and peppers, in the shade of the store, was decidedly unusual.

There'd been a twinkle in her eye, a casual set to her mouth, like she'd been willing him to say, "Ask me out already, cowboy." After staring into those eyes for too long—or not long enough, he considered—he'd actually gauged their particular shade of blue, like the ocean in the fading daylight, not quite sunset, waves turning in the breeze. That was the only comparison he could make. He thought on what it might be like to pull her into a kiss, place his hands on either side of her neck and draw close to those lips. Their eyes would fall closed and everything would happen by touch. Would it feel primal, the emotions shooting through him like a bolt of lightning? Or would it feel more like the slow burn of a good beer buzz?

Or better than anything he could ever imagine? Yeah, maybe he'd get that lucky.

He stepped inside the barn, found Mitchell and Rawlings conferring over a feed store receipt.

"There he is," Rawlings teased. "The man, the myth, the legend."

Brandt laughed and tapped the edge of his fist on the doorframe. "Would you mind if I spoke to my dad alone for a minute, pal?"

Rawlings shook his head. "Say the word, I'm gone." He slapped Brandt on the shoulder and headed out the door. Brandt noted his father evaluating him, and he tried to stand a little straighter. He sighed and moved closer to Mitchell, whose hands rested atop a wooden counter, his fingers playing with the edges of a clipboard.

"Dad?"

"I'm listening, son."

Brandt clasped his fingers together, then his hands fell to his side before he decided to hook one thumb in either pocket of his jeans. "I…" He glanced upward, as though he might find the answers on the ceiling of the barn, in stray splinters or bits of hay. "I'm going on a date tomorrow night and I just wanted to make sure it was okay with you."

Mitchell glanced thoughtfully at his only child, the one who bore a striking resemblance to him at the same age. "You're a little old to be asking my permission, Brandt."

Brandt yanked off his hat and knocked it against his thigh. Why did every conversation with his father feel like pulling teeth, so much effort just to have a simple conversation? Maybe it was because Mitchell *was* right—Brandt hardly needed his father's permission to do anything. Then he recalled something from college, the psychology of birth order and how only children related to their parents. That's it, he decided—I'll play the "only child" card again.

"Don't worry, Brandt. I've got things under control around here. Go out and have fun. But not too much, okay?" he added with a smile. Brandt felt a weight lift from his shoulders.

"Thank you, sir. I'll…I promise I'll get up early Saturday and do something. Anything you ask."

Mitchell leaned on both elbows atop the counter, bracing his body there. "Don't worry about it." He hitched his chin toward the door. "Go give your buddy an earful. You know he's dying to hear this conversation."

Brandt laughed. "Sure thing." He ambled back outside, found an anxious Rawlings leaning against the weathered red slats of wood that covered the barn. "How much of that did you hear?"

"None," Rawlings answered, breathless with anticipation. "Did you ask her out? Farm store girl?"

Brandt chuckled. "Marissa. And yeah, I asked her out. Tomorrow night."

Rawlings whistled, looked like he'd just won a first-place ribbon at the county fair. "Where you gonna go?"

He seated his hat atop his head and adjusted it like he was on the silver screen, one hand on either end of the brim. "I don't know yet, partner. You got any ideas for me?"

Rawlings's brown eyes rolled around in his head. "My idea of romance involves the bunkhouse and a case of beer." He smiled in self-chagrin. "That won't work for Brandt Conner, though. Gotta slap on some cologne. Slide some grease through your hair."

Brandt looked past him, toward the pasture where cattle grazed lazily, glassy-eyed and disinterested. "When was the last time you saw me with grease in my hair, McCoy?" His flat tone was betrayed by the smirk forming in the right corner of his mouth.

"Senior prom. You had a bolo tie and a blue vest."

"You're good," Brandt said. "That's not gonna work for tomorrow night. We already agreed to keep things casual."

Rawlings responded with a shit-eating grin. "Chivalry ain't dead. It's alive and well and goes by the name *Brandt*." And then he made those horrible mock-smooching noises that made Brandt want to laugh, smack him around a little, and then apologize.

"Mark my words," Brandt said, yanking his phone from his pocket and scrolling through until he found her number; her thumbprint on the screen caused him to smile. "Someday you will meet a woman who will make you wanna smooth out all your rough edges and be a better man."

Rawlings snorted. "Yeah, just so long as I don't start talking like you." He grinned. "Embarrassing, man. Just embarrassing."

Chapter Four

Brandt checked himself in the mirror. He made sure his shirt was tucked in and that his belt had snaked through every loop atop his jeans. He was broad-shouldered but pretty narrow at the waist. He locked eyes with his reflection, looked himself up and down, and wondered what a woman saw when she looked at him. He was classically handsome, even if he had inherited his father's weary expressions and smooth face. What he wouldn't have given, every now and then, for Rawlings's sharp nose, or maybe darker eyes. He angled his face away from the glass, glanced at his jawline. Well, plenty of women had been attracted to this face, so who was he to complain?

He didn't slap on cologne, as his best friend had suggested. Instead, he sprayed once in the center of his chest before he finished doing up the buttons. It wasn't like he'd be staring at himself all night. He was going to focus his attentions completely on Marissa—the lines and contours of her face, the shape of her body, the feel of her skin. If he even touched her, he had to remind himself. This was, after all, a first date, with someone he barely knew. Hell, he barely knew her last name.

His father was waiting for him at the bottom of the stairs. "Did you want to take the car, son? I'll give you the keys."

He shook his head. "The truck is fine, Dad." He scooped up his hat, held it against his stomach. "Maybe next time, okay?"

Mitchell smiled. "Drive safe."

"Always."

Out in the truck, Brandt leaned back against the headrest and took in a few deep breaths. "You can do this," he said aloud. "I can do this. This ain't my first rodeo."

• • •

Brandt parked behind the farm store, perpendicular to the wooden staircase and deck that looked a lot newer than the rest of the building. He hadn't thought to ask if there was more than one apartment upstairs, and was relieved to find out there wasn't. He steeled his nerves, snapped on his hat, and flew out of the truck before he had the chance to wimp out. His boots made a clunking sound on the steps, and he intentionally tried to soften his footsteps. It didn't work.

He lifted his right hand and formed a fist, holding it in the air for several seconds before he bothered to knock. He looked around, saw the deck had been stained but lacked any sort of furniture. There needed to be a potted plant stuck in the window ledge or something. Maybe he'd bring her one on their second date.

He knocked once, and had to swallow hard when she answered the door. She was a vision in blue, wearing a checked shirt and jeans, her eyes radiant in the last vestiges of daylight. "Hi, Brandt," she said, smiling brightly.

"You look beautiful," he said, the words escaping his lips before his better judgment could reel them back in. And for a moment, he was certain she'd blushed.

"Thank you," she replied, disarming him completely. If he hadn't already talked himself out of it five or six times on the drive over, he would've pulled her against his chest and kissed her until they were both gasping for air. And maybe a less mature Brandt would have, but the nervous-as-hell guy standing on her doorstep tonight was not quite himself.

He struggled to keep his eyes on her face, trying for the chivalry Rawlings had indicted him with earlier. Just a peek lower, his gaze dropping toward her chest and board-flat stomach. "Are you ready to go?" he asked, snapping himself back to attention.

"I am," she confirmed. She locked the door behind her and he motioned with his arm for her to lead the way downstairs. He held the truck door for her, tried not to leer as her slender frame decorated his passenger seat. When he was sure she was safely inside, he closed the door and made quick work of climbing in the driver's side and turning over the engine. "So where are we headed, Brandt?"

He laughed, and his eyes met hers briefly as they hit the main road. "It's a surprise," he said.

. . .

Marissa watched his fingers grip the steering wheel, the knuckles on both hands turning white. She smiled—men were so easy to read sometimes. He was definitely watching his step around her, his lips moving in a nervous tic, unable to find the words he clearly wanted to say. She wondered if he even knew he had such a telling gesture. She decided to save it for later. What he didn't know wouldn't hurt him.

He drove her to the other side of town, which wasn't a long trip during the day. In early evening, with minimal traffic, they arrived at the restaurant within a few minutes.

"I hope this is okay," he said, his hand resting on his door handle.

"It's fine," she assured him. "I'm new in town so everything is an adventure."

He laughed uneasily, the sound catching somewhere between his throat and tongue. "You're not from around here, are you?"

"Brackville."

"Tennessee," he said, and she caught the mild wince in his expression. "Bummer."

"It's not so bad," she asserted. Marissa was a woman who knew how to stand her ground. "Try not to hold it against me."

"There's something I'd like to hold against you," he muttered, "and that's not it." She smiled as he ducked out of the truck and made his way to her side, holding the door for her yet again. She could get used to this, this old-fashioned sense of respect, a man who possessed good manners but wasn't shy about the testosterone coursing through his veins.

As she and Brandt rounded the front of the truck, her boots scuffing the asphalt, she glanced back over her shoulder and said, "If you'd like to place your hand on the small of my back, feel free." He didn't take the hint, but she caught the brief, roguish grin that crossed his lips.

He was close on her heels as they entered the restaurant. The place had a nice ambience—the lighting was dim but not to the point a person couldn't read the menu. The benches and chairs were soft, and each table featured a vase of fresh flowers. Most of them were full, it being a Friday night. With snow assuredly gone for another season, people were coming out of their winter cocoons and reveling in the warmer weather. Marissa found herself grateful for the early spring heat—it'd put Brandt in her path twice in two days, and that was the sort of happy accident she'd needed for too long now.

They were seated at an intimate table for two near the back corner of the restaurant, where a window overlooked a small pond.

"Frogs." He must've followed her eyes to the pond, because he drawled out the word easily, as though it was a normal transition in the conversation. "Every summer they have to catch the frogs out of that pond because it gets so loud the servers can't even hear you order."

Marissa smiled at that, wondered if maybe he was pulling her leg. He removed his hat and rested it atop the table, and then trailed a few fingers across his scalp. His russet hair was cut in short, tidy strands, with a wave near the front to indicate an untamable cowlick. Again she was struck by the hue of his eyes, the mystery they seemed to convey. He gave her a small smile and she returned the expression as she flipped her menu open.

"So…what's good here?" she asked quietly.

"Pretty much everything," he answered, studying the menu as intently as if it were a textbook. "The catfish, the fried chicken… the steamed shrimp is choice too."

Good thing I'm not a vegetarian, she thought amusedly. Every dish was made with some form of meat, including a fair number of the side dishes. When the server returned, Brandt ordered fried chicken and Marissa sprang for the catfish. She took a sip of her water and glanced around the restaurant, taking in the sights and sounds. When her gaze returned to the table, she found Brandt watching her like a hawk.

"What's on your mind, cowboy?" she asked, lifting her chin in a curious manner. "Either you're a man of few words or you're just as nervous as I am."

He grinned, flashing her every damned tooth in his mouth. "A little of both, I guess." His expression turned austere. "Before things go any further between us, I wanted to be honest about something."

She crossed her arms in front of her and rested both elbows along the edge of the table. "I'm listening."

Marissa watched him take in a deep breath, then release it before he deigned to speak. "I dated Mona's daughter a while back, and it didn't end well. I know she's kinda your boss and I didn't wanna make things uncomfortable for you if the subject came up."

She didn't have to pretend to puzzle over his revelation. "You mean Britt?"

"Uh-huh."

She shook her head at him. "It may not be my place to state this, Brandt, but she doesn't have the best reputation. Her parents are probably a little blind to that, but that's the way parents usually are. Blind to their children's flaws. Anyway, if you say things ended badly, I can't imagine it was your fault."

"I appreciate that," he said, tapping his fingers on the table. "If you don't mind my asking, what brought you to Layton?"

A laundry list of reasons ran through Marissa's head, but she settled on the most basic, honest answer. "I needed a job. My mom is friends with Mona—no, I don't know why—and that's how I got my foot in the door. The past two years, since I finished college, have been wretched. No one would hire me and I couldn't get admitted to graduate school. Not exactly how I saw my life turning out."

He leaned back in his chair and made a clicking noise with his mouth. "I hear that. If I didn't have the ranch, I don't know what other practical application there'd be for my agriculture degree."

"I wouldn't have pegged you for the college type," she replied, although in her mind she felt like she'd found a kindred spirit, another person maybe unsure of his place in the world, uncertain about the future.

"I'm not," he contended. "But four years of college versus four years of my parents asking me why I'm not in college? I think I chose the lesser of two evils."

"Do you have any brothers or sisters?" she asked, not trying to seem nosy.

He shook his head. "Only child."

"Same here."

His eyebrows lifted at that. "It's a hard row to hoe sometimes," he said. "I don't know, maybe some kids like it."

"It was just me and my mom when I was growing up," Marissa admitted, buttering a piece of her dinner roll before chewing it slowly.

"Your dad wasn't around?"

"No," she answered, lowering the tone of her voice. "He sends a card every year for my birthday. He's somewhere in Ohio, but I've never actually met him. He left when I was a toddler. He's like an anonymous benefactor, you know?" she joked. Or tried to joke—Marissa didn't subscribe to the idea that you couldn't miss what you'd never had.

"How much do we ever know our parents?" Brandt wondered aloud. "Even when we live right under their roof?"

"That's a valid point," she replied, "but I wouldn't have minded the chance."

He gave her a light shrug. "My best bud, Rawlings, he's got four siblings and not a single one of them have a good relationship with their parents."

Marissa frowned. "Why not?"

"I don't know, aside from the fact that they had too many kids and got overwhelmed. He's lived with us since he was old enough to leave home, on our ranch. My parents love him like he's their own, so he's lucky in that respect." One corner of his mouth quirked. "I don't know—if I ever have kids of my own, I don't want them to have to wonder if I love them. I want them to feel safe and secure with me, know they can come to me for anything."

The food was delivered and their drinks were refilled. Brandt just looked at Marissa. She paused, wondering if something was wrong but then realized he was waiting for her to take the first bite. "Excellent," she said, letting the hot, flaky fish loll around on her tongue.

"Best fish in town," he said, "not counting what you can catch on your own hook."

She allowed them to eat for a few minutes before she reintroduced conversation. He'd already revealed more than she would have anticipated, and she found herself doing the same, feeling at ease in his company. "What you said before, about having children."

"I'm sorry," he said once he'd swallowed a bite of food. "That was probably a little forward of me. It's just…if I stick with the ranch, which I'm pretty sure is gonna happen, then marriage and kids seems like the step I need to take. That's what I've gotta plan for."

"Are you looking to settle down?" she asked, feigning disinterest. He stared at her for a moment, those green eyes daring her to ask something more.

"Yeah," he said with a smile. "I am."

Marissa had never seriously considered children, outside of the offhand assertion that she didn't want them without being in some sort of committed relationship. She didn't know enough about Brandt to seriously consider it, but the possibility definitely intrigued her. If nothing else, she'd just like to see him without his clothes.

"What's that look mean?" he asked. She looked up and found him grinning at her. She was mortified—what, exactly, had been swimming around behind her eyes, overtaking her expression? Was she blushing? Glassy-eyed and dreamy?

"How exactly did I look?" she inquired.

Brandt laughed. "Like you were thinking about dessert."

"Yes," she fibbed. "I was thinking about strawberry cheesecake."

"Hot damn," he said, flexing his knuckles together. "A woman after my own heart."

Marissa shot him a quick wink. "You have no idea."

• • •

Brandt wheeled his truck through the outskirts of town, one-handed. His right hand rested on the console, and he thought several times about offering it to her. This was, without question, the most mature he'd ever behaved on a first date. Thus far there'd been no groping, and mostly clean language with a few double entendres thrown in for good measure. The heat building inside him was unmistakable, but nothing he couldn't control. He worked up his courage before asking his next question.

"How'd you like to see something else before I take you home?" He glanced at her from the corner of his eye, was relieved when she quickly opened her mouth in response.

"Sure," she said. "What is it?"

He cleared his throat. "It's kind of a surprise. A secret."

"Is it safe?" she asked, her tone humorous but not mocking.

"About as safe as anything else." He turned and gave her a brief smile. He signaled just north of a small bridge and went left down a dirt road, its path taking them alongside a narrow strip of water, a creek that jutted off the river miles and miles up the highway. It wasn't quite sundown, and he was relieved they'd made it in time. At the end of the road, he pulled forward and backed into a place just near the water's edge.

"I didn't bring a bathing suit," she teased, glancing in her side-view mirror.

He laughed and felt his neck grow warm. "We're not swimming," he replied. "And even if we were, bathing suits are optional." He gave her his best grin and hopped out of the truck. She matched his pace on the other side of the truck bed, meeting him just as he lowered the tailgate. "Need me to help you up?" he asked hopefully.

"No," she said, sliding across the bed liner with ease. "I don't."

He let her easy rejection roll of his shoulders, smiling as he settled a comfortable distance from her. He knotted his hands together and listened to the sounds of a country night. Sure enough, frogs were hollering, but there was no wind to stir the grass. He stared at the sun, turned the shade of a blood orange, its roundness fracturing the sky into tiers of color—blue, purple, pink. It was perfection to his eyes—and the only comparable sight at that moment was the woman sitting next to him.

"This is my favorite place in the world." He pulled his hands apart and wrapped them around the top of the tailgate. "I love to come out here and watch the sunset—and sometimes, the sunrise." Rays of daylight shimmered atop the water, momentary flashes of gold. He angled his head to one side and their eyes met. They both smiled.

"It's a peaceful place," Marissa figured.

Brandt nodded languidly. "Yeah." His gaze found its way past the shadows, deep into her eyes, and his lips fell open in a curious expression. "You think there'll be a second date?"

Her expression was confident but also projected a certain vulnerability to him, as though she was giving him a window into her soul. "Definitely."

He made quick work of the road back to her apartment, his tires eating the asphalt. As the moon thumbed its way up the sky, he walked her up the stairs, stopped short of placing his hand on her shoulder.

She turned to face him, her eyes not quite meeting his. She'd already slipped her key in the door and it now stood ajar. "I had a great time tonight, Brandt. Don't let the three-day rule get in the way, cowboy. Call me tomorrow."

His mouth fell open in shock. "Will do, ma'am." Before he could react further, she grabbed him by the lapels and pulled his head close. Her lips hit his cheek, an utterly stunning, completely satisfying move. The ovoid imprint of her mouth caused his face to ignite, the flash of heat engulfing him in a split-second. She pulled back slowly, letting the heat radiate between them; he could feel it coming off her skin in waves.

"On our next date, wear that same cologne," she whispered just before she ducked inside the door. "It works in your favor."

He heard the lock click, and swallowed hard. He lifted one hand and then put it back down before he could form a fist. "Shit, shit, shit," he said in time to his feet on the wooden stairs. "I am screwed."

Chapter Five

Yesterday, before Brandt's date with Marissa, he and Rawlings had wrested an empty water tank into the back of Mitchell's truck. A narrow ribbon of creek ran across the ranch but stock tanks were placed strategically across the land to service the cattle when it got low or froze solid in the harshest part of winter. Brandt was on such a high from the night before that he was up early, attaching a hose to the city-fed water supply spigot and sticking the other end in the plastic tank until it was full. The truck sank infinitesimally on its shocks and struts, the heavy-duty pickup not groaning much under its weight. He stood alongside the truck bed and stared out into the pasture, the grass still dewy. He angled his head toward the bunkhouse. Rawlings was staggering out on unsteady feet, yawning as he tucked in his shirttails. He slapped a black hat atop his head and gave Brandt an early-morning smile.

"I didn't wake you, did I?" Brandt asked.

"No," Rawlings answered, yawning again. "Mitch put you out the door early?"

Brandt laughed, his throat gravelly. "Nope, I nearly beat him to the table this morning. Good night last night, man. Good night."

Rawlings groaned. "My evening consisted of a six-pack and some bad television. So don't boast too much."

Brandt checked the water level before answering. "We went for dinner, talked a lot about her family and why she's here." He stopped to clear his throat. "She's from Brackville."

"Crossing the border, is we?" Rawlings joked.

"Something like that. Anyway, I took her out to my secret spot after that and we watched the sun go down."

"I'm gagging, but go on."

"That was the end. I took her home and she pulled my face to hers and kissed me on the cheek. We said goodnight and I came home."

Rawlings shot him a dismayed look. "A kiss on the cheek? Was that enough?"

"Hell yeah, it was enough!" Brandt responded with uncharacteristic irritation. "It was hot, bud. I mean, just standing in that small amount of real estate with her, feeling the heat from her mouth. I didn't even touch her."

"No hand-holding? No backrubs, no copping a feel?"

"Sorry to disappoint you," Brandt said with a shrug. "I was better-behaved than I've ever been in my life."

Rawlings shot him a pointed look. "Want me to slap you around, take back your Man Card?"

Brandt set his jaw firmly. "Don't even think about it." His phone went off in his pocket and he moved quickly to answer it.

"*Carrying Your Love with Me?* That's your ringtone?" Rawlings chortled. "You really have got it bad."

Brandt gave him a sidelong glance. "Yeah, Dad? Okay, we can do that. Yeah? Okay. See you later."

"Anything wrong?" Rawlings asked as Brandt stowed the phone back in his pocket. Brandt shook his head.

"Just normal stuff. Dad wants us to check the heifer again."

"She's gotta drop that calf eventually," Rawlings said.

Brandt saw that the tank was full and turned the spigot off. He rolled up the hose and returned it to the barn. Rawlings followed in his footsteps. Brandt looked into the cow's melancholy eyes and tossed a handful of hay across the stall door.

"She looks fine to me."

"Same here," Rawlings said as he moved to the other side, where he took his hand and examined the cow's side. Brandt was a little taken aback by his friend's gentleness, though he shouldn't have been. Even the most abrasive person usually had their soft side, and vice versa. "Hope we don't need to get the vet out here."

Brandt worked quickly to reassure him. "Dad'll call him—just say the word. He depends on you."

"Mitch is probably the finest man I've ever known," Rawlings admitted. "Next to you, of course," he added with a glint in his eye.

Brandt laughed loud enough to startle the cow. "Come on, you rascal. We've got more animals to water."

"Sounds good," Rawlings said, following him back into the sunlight. "And you can tell me all about this woman who's got you over a barrel."

•••

"Thanks for calling me today. Otherwise, I might've had to clean my apartment."

Rowan laughed and set down the knickknack she'd been holding in an effort to find its price. She'd called Marissa earlier and asked her to meet at the local flea market. "I like a good bargain," she'd said over the phone. "Why pay ten dollars for a new book when a gently-used copy is only a dollar?" And Marissa had found no reason to argue with that logic—after all, she'd grown up in a single-income family. Now they whiled away the remainder of their morning, looking through booths, milling about long tables, and perusing shelves. Rowan had a few things in a basket, but Marissa remained empty-handed.

"Believe me," Rowan said, sweeping red hair confidently over her shoulder, "a bad day at the flea market is always better than a good day with the vacuum cleaner."

Marissa laughed. "Well, I'd have to agree with that assessment." Rowan fumbled through a stack of paperbacks but didn't see anything that piqued her interest.

"So how was your first week of work?" she asked, her eyes carefully scanning a selection of vinyl records.

"Pretty good, actually. I got both a paycheck and a date out of the deal."

Rowan turned to face her. "Tell me more, and spare no details." Marissa took in a deep breath and began.

"A few days ago, this cowboy limped into the store where I work."

"Why was he limping?"

"I didn't ask."

Rowan looked contrite. "Sorry for the interruption. What does he look like?"

"Very handsome. Brown hair, green eyes unlike anything I've ever seen before, square-jawed. Kind of tall, just muscular enough to fill out a shirt. Quiet sort of guy, doesn't say much. And when he does talk, he looks you straight in the eye."

"Sounds like he made quite an impression on you."

Marissa picked up a tablecloth and inspected it more closely before committing to buy it. "You could say that. He came into the store to pick up some electric fencing, and I'm sure this is going to sound crazy but something passed between us in that moment. I've dated before, of course, but such a strong attraction at first glance? I think that's kinda rare."

Rowan laughed. "Yeah, it is. Or it's lust, and that's usually not hard to read." She picked up an antique glass bottle, gave it a cursory inspection, and placed it in her shopping basket. "I'm really bad at this listening thing. Continue."

"The manager introduced us—his name is Brandt and his family owns a ranch near town. She made it clear that she has no use for him, but I was, of course, interested from the word go."

"I like that name," Rowan asserted. "Brandt. It just sounds kind of manly."

"He came back the very next day looking for tomato plants. Which sounds like the worst pickup line ever, only he really did buy several. He asked for my expertise and we talked for a little bit outside, and finally he asked me out on a date. He checked to make sure I was single. And, to be honest, even if I had been involved with someone else, it would have been hard to say no."

"He must be pretty sexy then," Rowan mused, "to make you toss aside the thought of monogamy."

"Well, maybe I exaggerated." She pulled to a stop and the two women stood face-to-face in a less-traveled corner of the flea market. "I took things very slowly. I let him hold the door for me, told him he could touch my back if he felt the need. And it was strange—he was so hesitant, and yet so obviously crazed with want. The whole thing was really romantic, though. We went out to eat and then watched the sunset together. It was unlike any date I've ever been on."

Rowan's eyes blinked with unhidden curiosity. "So what happened?"

Marissa exhaled and gathered her blonde hair up in one hand. "He never touched me. When we got back to my apartment, I pulled him close and left a kiss on his cheek. End of date."

"So who, truly, showed more restraint last night?" Rowan wondered aloud. "You, or him?"

Marissa pretended to consider her friend's question for a few silent moments. "Me. Brandt was trying to be a gentleman. I was just playing hard-to-get and enjoying the hell out of it."

"Men need that sometimes," Rowan surmised. "Not gamesmanship but a woman to show that she's both interested and in control." They resumed their march through the store. "So what about the second date?"

"I told him to call me today," Marissa replied. "If he doesn't, I won't be mad—I will, however, hold his feet to the fire."

Rowan laughed and shook her head. "I'm glad I ran into you in the grocery store, because it sounds like I'm in for one heck of a show."

. . .

Brandt watched, from a distance, as several of the cattle meandered toward the full tanks. At his side, leaning against the truck, Rawlings replenished himself from a bottle of water. In between lengthy stretches of quiet, the two men had discussed cattle feed, Marissa, calves, hay, and finally swung back to Marissa.

"So you gonna wait a few days and call her back?" Rawlings guessed.

"No, McCoy, not this time. This girl is a rule-breaker."

"Hmm." Rawlings's face turned blank. "What do ya mean, pal?"

Brandt looked at him and grinned before returning his gaze to the horizon. "I mean that the normal rules don't apply here, partner. One date was enough to let me know that I'd like to spend a lot more time with this girl, getting to know her, learning about her. Believe me, if the physical stuff comes into play, I'll be more than happy to go along with it—she's got a great body—but I'm not going to force anything on her. She's nice, man. Sweet and kinda tough. I know, it doesn't make sense."

"That love shit never makes sense," Rawlings said, finishing his water. "But it's usually a fun ride while it lasts."

Brandt laughed. "It's kind of like bull riding—a total adrenaline rush for the brief moment of time before you wind up head-first in dirt."

"Or something worse," Rawlings joked, each of them levering themselves back in the truck. Their day was only beginning—they'd make a circuit of the entire ranch before it was done, loading a few fallen limbs into the back of the truck and checking the water level in the stream. And when all of that was done, there was still inventory to be done back at the barn.

• • •

"We've gotta make this shopping a regular thing," Rowan declared. The women stood between their two cars, out in the parking lot.

"I don't know if my budget can handle it," Marissa countered, "but window shopping could work."

"Please!" Rowan joked. "You bought, like, next to nothing."

"Bad habit," Marissa said with a frown. "Comes from being unemployed for so long."

Rowan placed a hand on her shoulder. "I've been there. And I know it's hard, but things will get better." Their eyes met. "Hey, if you can't find your dream job, at least you've locked onto your dream man." She smiled. "Am I right?"

Marissa feigned indifference, then smiled too. "Maybe."

Rowan nodded, and they exchanged a quick hug. As each of them began to climb into their driver's seats, she stopped, look toward Marissa and asked, "Hey, if the dream keeps going…"

"Yeah?" Marissa replied, almost grinning.

"See if he's got a friend for me."

Marissa cocked her head to the side and lifted her eyebrows. "I'll see what I can do."

• • •

Brandt and Marissa's days, disparate in their overall goals, concluded at the same fixed point. Freshly showered, Brandt had flung himself over the bed before he dialed her number. "What are you doing?" was how he answered her greeting, his voice purposefully suggestive.

"I've got some laundry in the washer, and in the dryer, and I'm cleaning. It's amazing how quickly dust can settle in one place.

He laughed. "Tell me about it. Try living in an old house sometime. I think it creeps through cracks in the walls."

"Enough talk about dust and dirt," she said. "What are you doing, Mr. Conner?"

"Would you believe," he asked in a low voice, "that I'm getting ready for bed?"

"Seems kind of early," she teased. "Got your teeth brushed?"

He laughed again. "Yes, ma'am. And it was a busy day—Rawlings and I checked the herd, which took a while, and then we did some odds and ends around the place."

"Sounds slightly more interesting than my day."

He massaged his left shoulder, a dull ache penetrating the joint. "Your day would've been more interesting with me around," he said.

She gave him a flirty laugh. "And why do you say that?"

"Oh, I know how to make things interesting. Don't ever doubt that."

"I'll keep that in mind. So," she drawled, "Did you call for a reason, or just a bit of shameless self-promotion?"

"I owe you a date," he said, clearing a throat roughened by a variety of factors—arousal chief among them. "I wanted to see if we could shoot for Tuesday night."

"Well," she hedged, "I guess…that works for me."

"Could I take you out for a beer?" he asked evenly, a twinge of hope evident in his query.

"I could go for that," she answered quickly. "But I've gotta warn you—I'm not a cheap drunk."

Brandt swallowed hard. "I have no interest in trying to drink you under the table."

"That's too bad," she said in a mildly censorious tone. "Just think of the fun we could've had down there on the floor."

He was pretty sure she could hear the loud gasp of air he just sucked into his lungs—hell, Rawlings could probably hear it from a hundred yards away, out in the bunkhouse.

"Goodnight, Brandt," she said. "Sweet dreams."

"Goodnight," he managed to sputter out. His wrist dropped the phone alongside his face, and the huge gasp of air was expelled. This strange tenseness in his gut, this feeling of unease, was all due to Marissa—and he was enjoying every second of it.

Chapter Six

The server returned to their table. "You care to bring two more longnecks over here?" Brandt asked. She answered in the affirmative and he thanked her.

When they were alone again, Marissa watched him thumb away droplets of condensation from the empty bottle still in front of him. She sipped her beer and smiled at him. The jukebox was so loud that she strained to hear every other word, but so far it'd been worth it. They were still waiting for their entrées to be delivered. "Where was I?" he asked above the din of the restaurant, the clinking silverware and musical echo.

"You were talking about your dad," she recalled. She'd hung on his every word, not only because she loved to hear him talk but also because she envied anyone with a father present in their lives.

"Oh," he said, gratitude in his expression. "My mom says it's because we're too much alike, and maybe she's right. We've always butted heads and it's gotten worse the past few years since I graduated from college. He accuses me of brooding and, I don't know, being standoffish. But he's exactly the same. He won't speak unless he feels there's something worth saying. It pisses me off sometimes, Marissa. Just because I know all about the ranch doesn't mean I'm through learning from him, or being his son. I live under his roof, and I respect him, but I'd like a little more in return."

Marissa nodded. "I can't speak from firsthand experience, but there's a certain psychology that plays a role in even the strongest parent-child relationships. Our mothers carry us in their bodies, building a connection that is damned-near unbreakable. Our fathers, on the other hand, are always striving to form that connection once we're out in the world." Two fresh bottles of beer showed up, and she and Brandt clinked the tops together before taking the first drink. "I don't know if that makes any sense. In some families the connection between father and child winds up being the stronger one. Maybe it's nature versus nature."

"I think it makes a lot of sense," Brandt said, smiling as he nursed his bottle between both hands.

"You're a lot closer to your mom," she presumed.

Brandt nodded to let her know she was correct. "My mom is under the delusion that I'm perfect," he said with a shrug. "And maybe that's how it should be."

"My mother always pushed me to be my best," Marissa said, "if not perfect. Even though we didn't have a whole lot outside the basic necessities, she never wanted me to be satisfied with my lot in life. She wanted me to strive for something better."

"I think I'd like your mom." Brandt grinned. "And not just because she raised such a smart, funny, beautiful daughter."

Marissa felt herself blush—whether from the heat of his stare and his words or the alcohol, she couldn't say for certain. "When you say things like that, I wonder if you're not just trying to get into my jeans."

He laughed guiltily. "Hell, aren't you trying to get into mine?"

She blushed again, and when it had passed, lowered her face across the table, just a hairsbreadth away from his. "All in good time," she said. "All in good time." If he'd kissed her in that instant, she wouldn't have complained—but she didn't want their first kiss soundtracked by loud music and sliding plates of food. She pulled back and looked at his smile again, watching the subtle pulsing of his neck muscles.

She watched him gather up his courage, one thumb nervously rubbing the label on his bottle. "So, my buddy..." he said.

"Rawlings?"

"Yeah." Brandt smiled. "That's him." He gave her a wink that was barely noticeable in the dark. "I keep telling him you're new in town but there's a part of him that's just as hardheaded as me. He's been wondering if you might have a girl hidden away for him. Double dates and all that."

Marissa laughed at the bizarre coincidence. "You know, I may have just the girl for him."

His eyebrows knotted together in disbelief. "Really?"

"Yeah, really. He sounds like a sweet guy, but…"

"But you're wondering what kind of miscreant he'd have to be if he's my friend?" Brandt's tone was light and jocular.

"Of course!" she retorted, and they both laughed. "No, if he's your friend, I know he must be a good guy. I'd like to meet him myself, if that's okay—check to see if he's a good fit for her."

Brandt groaned. "I'll warn him away from embarrassing me with any and all stories about our childhood."

"Come on, you, a troublemaker?" Marisa teased. "I'm sure you got plenty of awards for good citizenship."

Brandt's face formed into one of those half-smiles, a mischievous look that was usually accompanied by a variant of the truth. But this time it quickly changed into a shamefaced grin. "I did get one of those," he admitted. "Rawlings was always more of a scrapper. It wasn't easy to learn how to cut the horns off a cow, but school wasn't too much of a struggle. I knew I had to grit it out and get it done."

"So you could get back to the ranch?" she guessed.

"Yeah," he said. His smile turned warm, a more genuine expression returning to his face. "Exactly."

•••

"Come on," Brandt challenged, dragging his last French fry through a dab of the ketchup. "There is no way you've seen *Pure Country* more times than me."

"That's where you're wrong, cowboy," Marissa said, shaking her head. "I watched it every day for two months. Wore out the DVD and the player."

"I watched it once a month while in college," Brandt countered. "Thank God I lived alone—there was no one to bitch and complain." He smiled at her—she was looking good and flushed, and somehow remained just as sober as he did. Damned food, getting in the way of his buzz. Then again, he was driving. They'd spent much of the previous hour discussing movies, music, college basketball, and food. "If I'd known you had such good taste in movies, I would've asked you out on day one."

"You showed great restraint waiting until day two," she answered. "Maybe your next stop is a monastery?"

Brandt laughed. "The vow of silence I could handle, but the vow of celibacy would be a deal-breaker." He examined her closely as she finished her meal. Marissa was teasing the hell out of him, and he was enjoying every last bit of it. And with a body like hers, he thought, celibacy would be an incredible waste. "You ready for me to get the check?"

Marissa nodded. "You're not disappointed by my lack of intoxication, are you?"

"No." He grinned and saw the reflection of light along her lashes, turning the ends gold. "If there's one thing I'm coming to understand about you, it's that you always keep your wits about you."

"My mother taught me never to take crap from anyone, especially a man." Marissa twined her fingers together and rested her chin atop them, her elbows balanced on the table. "She never said anything about kisses, though. Apparently those are okay."

"That's where the trouble always begins," Brandt countered, his eyes tracing the curve of her mouth, both lips unfettered by gloss or anything darker. "Kissing is dangerous."

"Are you speaking from experience, Brandt Conner? Are you the lady-killer everyone says you are?"

"Oh, yeah," he said, arching one eyebrow. "Lucky you caught me in one of my rare single weeks." When he laid his hand across the receipt to check the total, her palm enveloped it, her fingers coming to rest atop his. He felt the sizzle and pop of crackling energy, the strange sensation of familiarity that came when their eyes met. Her blue irises remained calm, remarkably steady in contrast to her now-trembling lips.

"If you're planning to hurt me," she said, "could you let me down easy now? It'd save both of us a lot of trouble down the road."

An unexpected sea of emotion washed though him when he saw the trace of vulnerability threaded across her steel armor. "You can trust me, Marissa. I have no interest in doing anything to hurt you, now or ever. Some discord is inevitable. I'm just trying to give us this time to get to know one another before we make a stronger commitment."

"It's just the two of us, right?" she asked, tightening her hold across his knuckles. "Monogamy?"

"Yeah," he answered with a smile. "I don't want anyone else." And every word of it was true. As much as he wanted to make love to her, have her naked under the sheets, under him, for now it was enough to place his hand over hers, feel the hum of blood flowing in and out of her veins.

She started telling silly jokes and he laughed at each of them, because coming from that gorgeous, shapely mouth, they all sounded brand-new and hilarious. And as he drove back to her apartment, he took stock of the lengthening sunlight, the days growing longer. As spring blended into summer, he could think of innumerable ways to fill the hours of daylight, and they all involved her.

• • •

"Would you like to come inside, Brandt?" Marissa was surprised at the words falling from her mouth, and he must've been too, because his handsome visage altered in confusion before he settled on a more muted expression.

"I'd better not," he replied, shaking his head. "You've got work tomorrow, and so do I."

Before she had time to react, his hand was lifting her chin upward. "Another time, beautiful." His mouth snapped onto hers, a light, searing pressure at first. Then his hands moved to either side of her neck, tangling in her hair as he deepened the kiss, her mouth parting easily in acceptance of his tongue. She clasped one hand over his shoulder, draped the other against his hip. Her body rocked into his, feeling the hardness, the restraint, the desire ready to unspool at a moment's notice. When her tongue danced against his, a moan escaped his throat and he pulled back swiftly, both hands still along the nape of her neck. She could hear his ragged breathing, saw with stark clarity the strange unease and unguarded want burning in his green eyes.

"I should really go," he said, the words coming out in gasps. He pulled her to him in an awkward half-hug, careful to keep their thighs from brushing. "Okay," he said flatly, bending to kiss the top of her head. "Goodnight."

"Goodnight," she said, their hands and forms sliding apart. She watched him descend the stairs, turning back to look at her at least twice before he drove away. She floated into the apartment on a cloud of air, her mouth still warm and buzzing from the after-effects of his simple act. It had been one hell of a first kiss, and if that's what she had to look forward to every time, she was more than ready for what he had to offer.

•••

Brandt pulled his truck to a stop in its usual spot, turned off the engine, and was jogging toward the porch when something caught his eye. Rawlings was seated in a chair near the door, barely a silhouette in the dim light. Brandt smiled and crouched alongside him. "Didn't expect to see you out tonight," he said.

Rawlings chuckled softly. "Wasn't sure I'd see you home so early, but I took a chance." He put one hand to his mouth to cover a yawn. "How was date number two?"

"It was great," Brandt told him. "We went for dinner and had a few beers."

"She outdrink you?" Rawlings asked with no small touch of admiration.

"Just about," he confirmed. He tapped one hand against the wooden slats of the floor, levered his tired body on shaky knees. "But the best part of the night was the kiss."

Rawlings slapped him gently on the shoulder. "I can remember a time when the best part of your night was everything but the kiss."

"Well," Brandt said with a nod, "I guess I'm maturing. Just a touch though. Don't want to scare you into thinking I've been replaced by an imposter."

"No, no," Rawlings answered. He glanced at his friend briefly and smiled. "I can see it in your eyes. You're really happy."

"It was really something, man. It wasn't just one of those 'this kiss will lead to great sex' things. It was the kind of kiss where you close your eyes and fireworks explode in your brain." He laughed. "And I didn't even mention the best part."

"Wait," Rawlings said, "there's more?" They both fell into crazy laughter.

"Believe it or not, Marissa wants to meet you. She wants to see what kind of wildcatter I'd pick as a best friend."

"Smart gal," Rawlings said with a nod. "And on that note, I'd better call it a night."

"Me too," Brandt said, getting to his feet. "Goodnight." He slipped his key in the lock and closed the door softly behind him. He tiptoed up the stairs, feeling pretty relaxed, at ease with the choices he was making in both his life and this new relationship. He undressed, fell into bed, checked his phone for messages, and drifted to sleep in a matter of seconds.

* * *

"The suspense is killing me," Josie said. "And I'm living vicariously through you, so spill." Marissa leaned back against the counter, looking up and down the aisles of the store. The place was dead, not one single customer having pushed through the front door in the past hour. Could've had something to do with the nice weather—who wanted to price seeds or grain on a spring day when the temperature was predicted to top seventy degrees? When she saw that Mona's door was open a crack, she withdrew her eyes and focused her words, at a whisper, on her enthusiastic coworker.

"There was a kiss," she admitted. "And not just any kiss, but the kind where your skin sizzles and your brain turns to mush."

"In my experience, those are about as common as four-leaf clovers." Josie smiled. "I'm jealous. Continue."

"Brandt and I have a lot in common," she said. "More than I expected, to be honest. I'm glad, though. He's got a great sense of humor but also pretty good manners. He'll say something sexy, but not insulting."

"Flattering," Josie clarified.

Marissa nodded. "Exactly." She lowered the tone of her voice even further now. "To be honest, I've had great sex with other guys. Lucky me. But I've never anticipated it as much as I am with

Brandt. It's crazy—just from the look in his eyes, an expression he may not even be aware of—well, it causes me to blush. Crazy, huh?"

"Anticipation is half the fun, isn't it?" Josie asked.

"Yes, but I hope it's not the only fun part." They laughed loud enough, then, to drown out the footsteps clapping along the floor.

"What are you two hens cackling about?" Mona asked sharply. Both women stiffened and resumed their at-attention clerk stances.

"Just the lack of foot traffic today, and some silly ideas to stir up business," Marissa replied.

"Like what?" the older woman asked pointedly.

"Maybe we need better signage," Josie recommended. "How do people know we have in sprouts if we don't advertise?"

Mona nodded, as though this was the best idea she'd heard all day. "Good initiative, you two. Just be sure not to scare away the customers with your laughing."

"We'll be sure to tone it down," Marissa promised. And, seemingly satisfied, Mona returned to her office, leaving them to enjoy laughter that was quieter but no less amused.

"Let's restock some shelves," Josie suggested. "Anything to keep the dragon lady off our backs."

"Sounds good," Marissa answered. "Maybe we'll even enjoy it."

Chapter Seven

Brandt awoke at his usual time, though an unusual sound broke through the silence of morning. He could hear a tractor out in the yard, plowing up rows in the garden. By the time he'd shaved, dressed, and made his way downstairs, the cacophony had ceased, but the kitchen was also empty. He found a plate of food in the oven and ate by himself, enjoying the peace and quiet. He heard a cow bellow in the distance, birds singing outside the window, and that was it. He found himself wondering if Marissa was at work yet, then remembered the store didn't open that early. They'd talked a little on the phone the previous night, made some plans for later in the week. It wouldn't be a date this time, with Rawlings coming along, but that was the way she wanted it. She was unexpectedly excited to meet his friend, and he couldn't help but love her enthusiasm.

Brandt ate hurriedly, then left his dirty dishes in the sink, scooped up his hat, and headed out the back door. The tractor rested alongside the barn, and his mother was counting seeds on the porch railing.

"Need any help?" he offered.

Laura glanced up at him and smiled. "I would love that, if you have the time. You can drop the seeds in carefully-spaced intervals before I cover them." She looked toward the sky, gauging the weather with both eyes. "I just hope there won't be a late frost this year."

Brandt stared at the lines of freshly tilled dirt, his lips pursed together. "Maybe you oughta drop the seeds and let me cover them. That's a lot of work, Mom."

Her blue eyes sparkled in mild rebuke. "I was planting this garden long before you came along, Brandt. I'm not ready to be put out to pasture just yet."

"I know," he answered with a nod. He spent the next half-hour a few steps ahead of Laura, judiciously setting potatoes and onions; corn, beans, radishes, and cabbage would come later. Thanks to the beef cattle, Mitchell and Laura could easily afford to shop at a supermarket, buy fruits and vegetables trucked in from someone else's farm. However, they'd impressed upon their son at an early age the importance of taking what the land provided and subsequently finding a way to give something back. It had been standard practice from the time he was old enough to wield a hoe and rake: plow the garden in the spring, rake up the leaves in the fall. Even Rawlings had been put on seed duty from a young age, not that he ever complained. It didn't matter what task they were drafted into; as long as he was at Brandt's house, he'd help to complete it. Brandt looked toward the bunkhouse and smiled. Some things never changed.

"So when am I going to meet this girl you've been sparking?" Laura asked after a lull in the conversation. The metal end of the hoe scraped against a small rock. She picked up the stone and lobbed it toward the porch.

Brandt burst out laughing. "Do they still call it 'sparking,' Mom?"

"No," she responded with a knowing smile, "but I do."

"Her name is Marissa," he said, "and I'm sure she'd love to meet you. She wants to meet Rawlings too, so we're going to hang out later this week."

"She sounds special, if you want her meeting your best friend."

"She is, Mom." Brandt perched himself atop the rake and smiled. "This is definitely the beginning of something good."

Laura gathered her long brown hair into a bun and pinned it atop her head. "Your father said you met her at the farm store?"

He nodded. "She just moved up here from Tennessee. Hope you're not disappointed I didn't pick someone from your church."

"Not at all," she said, smiling warmly. "Your happiness is my only concern."

"And Dad?" he asked pointedly.

Laura continued to smile. "Your happiness is also his primary concern. He just has a different way of showing it."

Brandt opened the corner of a bag of fertilizer and poured it evenly atop the potatoes. "You'd both like a few grandchildren, huh?"

Laura wiped at her forehead with one exposed wrist. "That would be nice, although you're still young. You have plenty of time."

When Brandt was younger, time had seemed endless, and he'd wondered if he'd ever grow up. Somewhere along the way, time sped up—college was over in the blink of an eye, his grandparents and much of their generation had passed away, and his parents had grayed, lines settling into the corners of their eyes. He no longer looked forward to his birthday, which rolled around quicker each year. Getting married and starting a family of his own had always seemed like a fixed point in the future, a goal to strive for, something that would click into place like a key turning in a lock. As he got older, he began to realize that didn't make much sense—love happened on its own time, and while you might help it along, you could never quite predict or plan for it. Marissa was definitely proof of that.

•••

"I want you to be on your best behavior, McCoy."

Rawlings unleashed a laugh from deep in his gut. "Brandt, I was born on my best behavior."

"And it was all downhill from there." Brandt tapped his fingers against the steering wheel as he came to a stop sign. He looked both ways and headed on his journey, toward the restaurant he and Marissa had decided on the previous evening. He had to rein in some of his baser impulses when they spoke on the phone; there were things he wanted to say and do, but he tended to edge around them like a climber skirting the edge of a cliff. Marissa was far from delicate, but they were still feeling out the beginnings of a new relationship. The slightest thing could undermine them if Brandt didn't practice exceeding care. The whole business was foreign to him—he'd never been scared of anything in his life, save for his father and snakes, and he could dispatch of the latter with one twelve-gauge shell.

"Can I tell stories?" Rawlings asked like a kid begging to go inside a candy store.

"Yes," Brandt said with some resignation. "Try to avoid middle school, though."

"But that's where the best stuff comes from!" he argued. "Like the time we broke the heater in the locker room."

"That was an accident," Brandt recalled, "and we've also managed to keep it under our hats for the better part of twelve years."

"Yeah, well, when the toilet blows up," Rawlings figured, "everything else gets overlooked." Brandt smiled at the memory, a prank neither he nor Rawlings could take credit for. They had only been troublemakers in the broadest sense of the term, just providing enough levity to get them through the tedium of life at a small-town school. And if Rawlings hadn't been as successful in some subjects as Brandt, they always seemed to find a way to study together that was mutually beneficial when report cards came around.

"You can tell her about the good old days," Brandt declared, finally relenting, "but try to keep them on the legal side."

Rawlings, who'd been staring out the window, turned his head toward Brandt and smiled. "Deal."

• • •

Marissa tapped a few fingers absently against the planed wooden surface of the table. She'd arrived at the restaurant first and secured a booth for them. She was a little anxious, but mostly excited about meeting Brandt's best friend. She'd talked to her mother for a little while earlier in the evening, and Connie Sloan had been pretty interested in her daughter's boyfriend—maybe a little too interested. What was it about parents that made them want to rush their children into settling down? Marissa frowned. Perhaps it was them realizing their own mortality and wanting to leave children behind who were loved, secure, happy. Or in Connie's case, wanting better for Marissa than what she'd had.

"My prodigal father," Marissa whispered to herself. "It always comes back to you." She glanced around and saw Brandt's familiar lanky figure cutting though the restaurant. As he drew close, she took stock of his companion—not quite as tall as Brandt, but thicker across the chest, with dark hair and dark eyes. He had an attractive face, with a natural friendliness that shone through in his expressions. She stood to greet each of them. Brandt left a kiss on her cheek—it was appropriate under the circumstances, but she yearned for a little more.

"Rawlings McCoy," he said, extending a hand. "Pleased to make your acquaintance, ma'am."

"Marissa Sloan," she said, shaking his hand and providing her best smile. "I feel like I know you already." He seemed to blush slightly as they took their seats.

"Now that I've seen you," Rawlings began, "it makes me wonder what such a pretty girl would be doing with a knothead like Brandt."

"Take it easy," Brandt murmured, his shoulder rubbing against Marissa's. She linked arms with him and twined her fingers through his.

"I find Brandt to be very handsome," she said smartly, "and more than a little bit sexy." Her thumb lingered over his palm, feeling the skin grow warm.

Rawlings laughed. "You shoulda seen him back in middle school."

"It starts," Brandt said to no one in particular as Rawlings continued his trip down Memory Lane.

"His growth spurt didn't take off all at once, so for a while his arms and legs didn't match the rest of his body. He was like one of them Neanderthal drawings from before humans could walk upright."

Marissa rested her head against Brandt's shoulder for a moment before she forced him to meet her eyes. "Is that true—did you have trouble walking upright?"

Brandt winked at her. "Guilty as charged, ma'am."

"What do we gotta do to get some beers around here?" Rawlings asked, his eyes darting around the restaurant.

"I told our server to keep them coming once you arrived," Marissa announced.

"Good," he said, grinning, "because I can drink the two of you under the table any day of the week."

"I doubt that," Marissa challenged him amiably, "but not tonight, because I have to drive home."

"How is work going?" Brandt asked softly, shelling a peanut before tossing it in his mouth.

"My co-workers are all great," Marissa answered, "with the exception of Mona."

"She's just miserable all the time," Brandt said. "Don't let her get you down."

"No excuse for the woman to act like that," Rawlings complained. "She has a great husband, and great kids. Not counting Britt, anyway."

"I've found ways around it," Marissa pointed out, thinking back to earlier in the week when Mona had invited her to church. She'd politely declined, with the excuse that she was still trying to get settled in, find her bearings in Layton. All of that was true, but she also enjoyed her personal time, even if she and Brandt were spending part of it on the phone each night.

The beer finally arrived, and they tapped their bottles together. "To Brandt and Marissa," Rawlings toasted. "You guys make a great-looking couple."

"In case you hadn't noticed," Brandt said, placing his bottle to his lips, "Rawlings is about as subtle as a jackhammer."

"Oh," Marissa said, giving her new friend a wink across table, "that seems to be one of his many great qualities."

He smiled at her in gratitude, rubbing condensation from his bottle. "What'd I tell you, Brandt? Any girl that dates you *must* have great taste."

At one point during the meal, Brandt excused himself to the restroom. He kissed Marissa lightly on the lips and jokingly told Rawlings to behave. When it was just the two of them, he glanced across the table, his jocular face turning serious.

"Hope you don't mind, but Brandt told me your dad wasn't around."

She nodded. "And he told me you weren't close to your family at all."

He frowned, but nodded in the affirmative. "I'm lucky to have Brandt. His dad, Mitch, is the best, and his mom is amazing too. My parents…I don't know." Both eyes lowered to the table as he rotated an empty bottle between his hands. "Maybe they were overwhelmed by the farm, or having too many of us kids, but they just couldn't provide any of us with the time and care we needed. Now we're all pretty much scattered and don't really talk."

"That's sad," Marissa said, understanding his pain. "It was always just my mom and me, but she gave me enough love for ten parents." She smiled warmly at him. "I don't get jealous, Rawlings, but Brandt talks about you an awful lot. You're more like his brother than his friend."

He shrugged at her assertion, but the ghost of a smile formed upon his lips. "Well, maybe. He's a good guy, Marissa. What you see is what you get. He can be a little showy at times but there's nothing hidden. Only person he hides from is his dad, and you and I have enough father issues ourselves without trying to dissect his."

Marissa laughed and aimed her bottle at him. "Damned straight."

Brandt returned to the booth and slid in next to her, resting one hand atop her leg. His fingers caressed the impression of her knee that he found through her jeans. "What'd I miss?" he asked, tossing some food in his mouth.

"Too much," Marissa joked. "We weren't sure how to break the news to you, but Rawlings and I are best friends now."

Rawlings nodded in accord. "I'll head down to the drugstore tomorrow and see if they make a card for this occasion."

Brandt shook his head, a huge grin affixed to his mouth. "You two," he chided. "I might've known you'd get along like a house on fire."

"Just wait," Marissa said, looking from one to the other, "until we have a real drinking contest. You'll both hate me."

Brandt brushed his mouth across her cheekbone, sending a shard of heat through her body. "That would never happen, beautiful."

• • •

Rawlings wheedled until they agreed to let him take care of the bill, not that Brandt did much protesting. In the dusky air, behind the shade of his truck, Brandt pulled Marissa into a series of kisses, each one deeper than the last. He let his hands linger gently, then sensuously, over the curve of her back and hips. Then she surprised him by undoing a button low on his shirt and sliding her fingers against his stomach. The touch of her hand anywhere on his skin was enough to send his mind into a daze. The thought of her palm, her nails, her fingertips anywhere else on his body took over, centered itself in his core, and they were too tightly clenched together for her not to feel it too.

"Can't control yourself, can you?" she joked, nearly out of breath.

He laughed with no small measure of chagrin. "Guilty as charged."

"Hmm," she said, sliding fingers past his belt and along the waist of his jeans. "Save it for a rainy day." Her blue eyes were mischievous, almost sparkling with wicked heat, as she met his gaze. He tried not to groan as they made the quick walk back to her car, and they kissed one last time before he closed the door firmly behind her. He was walking away when she rolled down the window and yelled for him to stop. He turned at the waist, and glanced back over his right shoulder. "It's springtime," she pointed out. "There'll be plenty of rainy days." He grinned back at her as she did the same, and he watched her drive away into the night. He was still frozen in place when Rawlings, his shirt pocket full of peanuts, ambled into the parking lot.

"Crap," he said, thumping a few fingers against the brim of his hat. "I was gonna tell her goodnight."

"Don't worry," Brandt said, turning to smile at his friend. "You'll be seeing her again."

Chapter Eight

"He's definitely a hunk." Rowan examined the photo Marissa had taken on her cell phone before handing it back to her. Marissa scrolled to the next photo.

"This is his best friend, Rawlings."

"Wow," Rowan said, her eyes widening. "He's kind of a hunk too. Where have you been hiding these guys?"

Marissa laughed and shook her head. "Hey, I just met them myself. Apparently they've been hiding themselves out on the ranch, to which I have to say, 'Lucky us.'"

"Do you think he and I would hit it off?"

"Oh, definitely," Marissa confirmed. "I noted a lot of similarities in your personalities. Neither of you has much of a tolerance for bullshit, although he can freely dole it out with a gleam in his eyes."

Rowan had been gnawing on the remnants of an ice cream cone, and paused long enough to wipe her mouth. "Did you tell him I was interested?"

"Not in so many words." Marissa adjusted her sunglasses, and glanced across the park where they'd rested themselves on a bench. "But approximately five minutes after Brandt and I started dating, he inquired about whether or not I had a friend so we could double date. Apparently it was God's plan that you and I would reconnect after all this time. Or just dumb luck." A light wind blew through the park, lifting the blades of grass upward. "Nothing is set in stone yet, but you and I are available pretty much every night."

"Somehow I get my papers graded during my free period at school," Rowan asserted. "So my nights and weekends, for the foreseeable future, are free for any and all dating. And summer, aside from planning, is totally open to possibilities."

Marissa smiled. "Sounds good. A word of warning, though…"

"Uh-oh," Rowan said caustically.

"They're boisterous when you put the two of them together, but otherwise they give new meaning to 'the strong, silent type.' Honestly, Brandt and I had an instant attraction but I think he had to force the words out of himself. Rawlings is a little better—he talked to me without any prodding."

"Where does he live?" Rowan asked, taking a sip from her cup of ice water.

"On the ranch with Brandt. Technically he's out in the bunkhouse, but he's part of the family." Marissa sighed. "I'm headed out there soon, myself. My first dinner with Brandt's parents."

Rowan nodded. "Sounds serious."

"It is." She swallowed nervously. "I just want them to like me, you know? Especially if Brandt and I are going to have any sort of future."

"I completely understand." Rowan shot her a reassuring smile. "You want any potential in-laws to like you."

"I'm going to try my best to make them like me," Marissa promised. "Especially Brandt's father. I have a sneaking suspicion he will be the tougher sell."

• • •

Brandt stared at his clipboard, then read the items matter-of-factly. "Cattle feed."

"Cattle feed," Rawlings repeated in the same dry tone.

"Fertilizer."

"Fertilizer."

"Lime."

"Lime."

Brandt glanced downward and smiled. "Straightjackets."

"Fitted for each of us," Rawlings quickly responded. They smiled at one another and laughed.

"Just threw that one in to make sure you were paying attention, bud," Brandt apologized. "Joke's on me, then."

"Nah, you're not wrong. I was drifting there for a minute." He gave the interior of the barn an appraising glance. "Lot of things on my mind these days."

Brandt folded both arms across his chest and leaned back against the workbench. "Anything you'd care to talk about?"

Rawlings shook his head but decided to speak anyway. "I'm thinking about where things stand with us while you and Marissa get more and more serious."

Brandt frowned instinctually, though he'd intended his answer to be reassuring. "Look, man, you've got a home here as long as you want it. If you decide to settle down…"

He laughed. "Fat chance, I know…"

"…we'll add onto the bunkhouse or build you a complete new place," Brandt continued. He made a fist, tapped the edge of it against his mouth. "Have you talked to Dad about this?"

"Mitch said pretty much the same thing as you," Rawlings conceded.

Brandt smiled. "Then what are you so worried about?" He lifted one eyebrow. "We're still gonna be best buds after one or both of us get married. Nothing will change in regard to that, but it will be an adjustment."

"She liked me, right?"

"Marissa?" Rawlings nodded. "Yeah. She thought you were great. And as soon as she can get it scheduled, we're going to double date."

Rawlings's brown eyes lit up at that. "Can't wait. And speaking of date, you looking forward to tonight?"

Brandt pondered the question for an eternity, but nodded anyway. Mitchell and Laura had anxiously sought a meeting with their son's girlfriend, perhaps because this was Brandt's most serious relationship in quite a while. The last girl—or maybe, he thought with some chagrin, the last three—hadn't really been meet-the-parents material. Marissa, on the other hand, was a different story, and contrary to the butterflies in his stomach, he looked forward to tonight, and hoped his parents would love her as much as he did. Brandt had fallen so hard and so fast that he imagined them being a little skeptical, though that would all change as soon as they got to know her.

"Yeah," he admitted. "I'm definitely looking forward to it."

When their work was finished for the day, Rawlings slapped him on the back as a good-luck gesture, and they said their goodbyes. Brandt went into the house, showered, and tossed on a little cologne. Maybe too much, he thought grudgingly. He headed into town to pick up Marissa, having already decided it would be easier, and less stressful, to have her first trip out to the ranch mitigated by him. And there was an ulterior motive in mind, though he'd work his way up to that one.

With the abundance of nice weather, and the usual Saturday cruising, his short trip took a little longer than he'd planned. Finally he pulled up outside her apartment, climbed out of his truck, and took the steps two at a time. He was breathing hard by the time he knocked on her door, and felt himself thrown for a loop when she opened it a few seconds later.

Marissa's usual board-straight locks had been transformed into a series of golden waves that framed her face perfectly and fell gently against her shoulders. The Western shirt covering her upper body, light blue with subtle stripes of small pink flowers, brought out the luminous hue of her eyes. Her lips carried just enough red to draw attention to them—not that his mind wasn't already prone to thinking about her mouth.

"Damn," he said, and she smiled. "I mean, I'm sorry. You just look beautiful, Marissa." He reached for her hand and massaged her knuckles tenderly. "Really. I may not be able to take my eyes off you all night."

She stepped closer to him and the heat built in the narrow space that remained. "That cologne," she murmured. "You know what it does to me, don't you?"

Brandt wasn't entirely sure, but he had a pretty good idea. "Let's go, Miss Sloan." He pulled her fingers to his mouth and kissed the tips. "Your chariot awaits."

As he helped her into his truck, Brandt was increasingly unsure how he was going to get through this evening. His brain—not to mention parts further south—was firing on all cylinders. He took a few deep breaths, climbed into his truck, and started the engine.

• • •

Marissa took particular note of his demeanor on the drive out to the ranch. He was extra-quiet, barely uttering two syllables per sentence as the miles passed. Finally they turned into the driveway, and she was pleasantly surprised. There was a large barn, and what she figured must be the bunkhouse, but otherwise the only building she saw was the home Brandt shared with his parents. It was no mansion, but definitely an old farmhouse, indicated by its peeling paint, large windows, and front and back porch. The garden Brandt had told her about must've been out of view, she thought, her suspicions confirmed as they pulled to a stop and she got an eyeful of its neat, manicured rows. Annuals bloomed in pots placed here and there, and in the distance she saw a herd of cattle basking in the last rays of the sunlight. It was immediately clear why everyone who inhabited this place loved it—it carried a tranquil sense of home, of belonging, of contentment. She knew the cattle were a lot of hard work, but for this piece of land, they'd be well worth it.

"It's a beautiful place," Brandt said, echoing her thoughts. He shut off the engine and pocketed the keys. "Not as beautiful as you, of course, but it's home." He rounded the truck and took her hand in his, giving it a good squeeze. His grip strengthened as they hit the front porch and cleared the threshold. All at once she was inside the house, its bones squeaking as floorboards crackled beneath them. "You go to bed at night, the place quiets down some," he explained. "But as long as a person is walking around, the walls talk back to them."

"No wonder you don't talk much," she teased, leaning into him. She watched his eyes sweep over her.

"I talk to you," he countered.

"You're very good with words," she complimented, "and I am very thankful for that."

"Showtime," he said as they entered the living room. The house had a cozy, lived-in feel. Some of the furniture was noticeably worn, but not shabby. She figured the couch and chairs had undergone some reupholstering at least once in their life. From a recliner, a man in his early fifties rose to greet them. Marissa recognized him as Brandt's father immediately. Were it not for the weathered lines around his eyes and etched into his forehead, and the grey strands in his brown hair, Mitchell and Brandt were twins. Even their eyes were similar in color and shape. Marissa wondered if Brandt had inherited anything from his mother.

"Mitchell Conner," he said in a time-roughened voice. "Welcome to our home, young lady."

She shook his hand. "I'm Marissa," she said quickly. "It's nice to finally meet you."

"If it were up to me," he said in a friendly tone, "Brandt would've brought you around sooner. He has to do things in his own time, this one does." Marissa didn't feel it was her place to correct him—she and Brandt had just started dating. She felt Brandt stiffen beside her, and for the first time the difficult relationship between father and son manifested itself. She shot a sidelong glance toward the built-in shelves, lined with photos of Brandt and his high school diploma. Pride was evident, to be sure, but she knew as well as anyone the landmine-fraught relationship between father and child.

"I was waiting for the right time," Brandt answered in a brittle tone, "and this is it."

Mitchell nodded briefly, then returned his attention to Marissa. "Come with me, young lady. Brandt's mama is eager to meet you too."

As they wound their way back into the entry hall on Mitchell's heels, a beautiful woman came into view. Her face was lined similarly to her husband's, projecting wisdom and confidence onto the room. Her hair was a multi-colored affair, naturally reddish-brown with streaks of silver twined throughout. Brandt was definitely a product of her, though her eyes were a brilliant blue in contrast to his green. "Welcome to our home," she said to Marissa. "We are so pleased to have you here. I am Brandt's mother, Laura." She looked to her son briefly. "You told us she was beautiful, but you forgot to mention she was this lovely."

Marissa watched Brandt's neck redden before he took a second to compose himself. "Sorry, Mom. I'm a master of understatement."

"You brave girl," Laura said, resting a hand on her shoulder. "Tackling the strong, silent type. You'll win every argument you ever have with Brandt, because he can't spare the extra words."

"Don't scare the young lady off, Laura," Mitchell said affectionately. A smile briefly touched his lips. "She did come here to eat, after all."

"Oh!" she exclaimed, as though she'd struck gold. "I just put dinner on the table. Follow me."

Brandt led them through the door and helped Marissa into her seat. The heel of his palm intentionally grazed her shoulder, and something roared to life deep inside her. Brandt smiled at her gently, as though he hadn't just thrown her off balance. She folded a cloth napkin in her lap, focusing her attention on Brandt's parents. The meal was chicken pot pie, the homemade kind with handcrafted lattice covering the top, baked to a golden brown, looking like something from the cover of a cookbook. Oddly enough, after everyone dug through it and the accompanying salad, there still seemed to be plenty left over.

"Would you like any more sweet tea?" Laura asked softly. Marissa had liked her straight off. She was genuinely sweet, warm and welcoming, treating Marissa more like an old friend than someone she'd just met.

"Thank you," Marissa said. She watched Laura pour more for each of them from a pitcher, without bothering to ask either her husband or her son. Some things were just instinctual.

Mitchell cleared his throat. "Brandt tells us you're a college graduate, Marissa."

She nodded. "I have a degree in psychology, but I've never been able to put it to work. I used to dream of being a counselor, helping adolescents cope with the changes to their lives. It's such a critical time for all of us but there's so little guidance during that stage of development."

"I'm trying to convince Marissa to go back to school, rejections be damned, and work her way toward it," Brandt said, focusing his eyes on her. "She's definitely had a positive effect on me."

"You moved up here from Tennessee?" Laura asked.

"Yes, and I love it here so far. Just like back home, the people are very friendly. I might have to stay here permanently."

"How do you feel about cows?" Mitchell asked deliberately. "Specifically beef cattle."

"Dad," Brandt groaned.

"I love animals," Marissa replied. "And what is life without a little hard work?"

"She's a keeper," Mitchell, smiling broadly now, said to his son. "Better hang onto her."

"I intend to," Brandt said flatly.

In what Marissa realized later was a strategic, familiar move, Laura defused the situation in five seconds flat. "Who'd like some dessert?" she asked.

"What is it, Mom?" Brandt asked, feigning disinterest.

"Blueberry pie," she announced. "I froze the berries myself last year, and they taste as good as if they were fresh. There's also homemade whipped topping."

"I'll take half the pie, if you don't mind, sweetheart," Mitchell said, his eyes twinkling and mischievous, "and cut a few slivers for the kids and yourself."

"You jokester," Laura said, waving him off. "I'll come back with one slice for everybody." She disappeared into the kitchen, leaving untenable silence behind when she stepped through the swinging door.

"Mr. Conner?"

He looked across the table and smiled. "Yes, Marissa?"

"You and your wife raised a fine son. I've rarely met someone our age with better manners."

Something imperceptible flashed through his eyes before he settled on a more impartial gaze. "You're a very kind young woman, yourself. I'm glad Brandt found you."

"Me too, Dad," Brandt said. "Me too."

Laura returned momentarily with four saucers of pie, warm and fragrant, piled high with whipped cream. "I'm not one to brag," she said, "but this is a county fair winning recipe."

"She's right on both counts," Brandt confirmed. "This is amazing, award-winning pie, and she doesn't know the meaning of the word 'brag.'"

"I brag enough for the both of us," Mitchell said, fork slicing to the bottom of his plate. "I married the most beautiful girl in Layton, and she's a great cook to boot."

"I was not the most beautiful girl in Layton," she countered, "though when we married, I was certainly the happiest." Marissa watched as Brandt's parents shared a private moment. "Anyway," she said, returning her attention to her guest, "I have often said that you can't have a strong marriage without at least one spouse being a great cook. In some families, that's the husband. You'll be glad to know that I taught Brandt how to boil water years ago."

"Which is why I'm great at pasta," Brandt joked. "And little else."

"I'm fine with that," Marissa said, resting her hand atop his. "Who doesn't love spaghetti?"

As dessert was finished, and Marissa helped Laura with cleanup, she found security in the knowledge that she'd made a good first impression on two wonderful people who'd raised a great son, the man that she loved. Yes, loved. When Brandt excused himself for a moment and Laura pulled her into a hug, she realized she had found more than just a boyfriend, husband, or life partner. She'd found a second family. Mitchell shook her hand and waved them goodbye, and before they even left the driveway she found herself looking forward to her next visit.

Chapter Nine

Brandt eased his foot off the gas pedal, and told himself that he wasn't speeding. He was absolutely, one-hundred-percent not speeding back to her apartment. He glanced down at the speedometer—dammit. Those things didn't lie.

A mixture of relief and anxiety swept through him, accompanied by a rush of air from the open window. He was relieved his parents had taken to Marissa immediately. Laura had been a certainty from the beginning, but for Mitchell to have liked her? That was like winning the Kentucky Derby with a mule. Mitchell hadn't liked anyone Brandt had dragged home in years—Rawlings had been the last one—and so this was a huge step. Still, his father had needled him subtly during the meal, making comments that would only be offensive toward a son's attuned ears. And his anxiety? Well, that could only be taken care of one way—and depending on his stamina, maybe two or three ways.

He walked alongside her up the staircase, willing to say goodnight but hoping he wouldn't have to. As her key turned in the lock, she gave him a brief smile and asked, "Would you like to come inside?"

He nodded and followed her past the doorway, closing the door calmly behind him. The furniture inside was attractive and matched, and likely purchased with both eyes on a budget. She pointed toward the couch.

"You can sit down, if you'd like."

He thought on it for a few seconds, then answered, "I'd rather stand, if it's all the same to you." She nodded in reply.

"Would you like anything to drink?" He shook his head, then made a slight motion for her to step closer. Her eyes widened infinitesimally, a reaction he managed to see in the dimly-lit space.

"Marissa," he said hoarsely, something unspoken hanging in the air between them.

"Yes, Brandt?" she asked.

"I love you," he rasped, meeting her eyes steadily. "I love you, Marissa."

She gave him a closed-mouth smile. "I love you too, Brandt."

He cleared his throat twice, which was necessary as her words sank in. She'd provided them without hesitation, without any uncertainty in her voice. Her tone and expression emboldened him, a man who was scared of very little. Here in the moment, though, apprehension gripped his limbs.

"If you're still not ready, I'll understand. But I would like to be with you tonight, if only for a few hours." He looked away for a moment, fixed his eyes on the point where her carpet disappeared beneath the television console. He sought out resistance in her eyes. "I know it's pretty soon."

She stepped toward him, rested her hands atop his shoulders. "I wanted you pretty much from the word 'go,' Brandt. I thought I deserved a little better than that, of course, and as I got to know you over these past few weeks, I realized you did too." Her lips brushed his, and heat surged through his veins. "Did you bring anything?" He nodded and patted his shirt pocket. "You didn't have that in your shirt during the entire dinner, did you?" she asked, clearly amused.

He laughed out loud. "No, no, although that would've made a funny story."

She smiled and pressed her lips to his jawline, her breath torrid against his face, desire arcing through him. "I've been on the pill for quite a while," she assured him, "so we'll be twice as safe. You don't have to be nervous. I want this too."

"Who's nervous?" he asked, feigning offense.

"Both of us," she stated flatly. She took his hand then and pulled him easily toward the bedroom, the simple touch of her fingers enough to make him burn a little hotter inside. He followed her through the darkness, the room suddenly illuminated as she switched on a bedside lamp. The room was painted a pale, cool blue, looking like the sky on a tranquil autumn morning. She turned into his arms and her hands went for his shirt, undoing the buttons with ease. Both hands slid beneath the fabric, around his waist, skimming along his spine, finding the place where beads of sweat had begun to form. She pulled tight to him and he felt her breasts straining through the fabric of her shirt—or maybe that was the surface of his chest, the hard muscles struggling to feel her. She chewed on his lower lip, pulled it between her teeth. His palm moved along her back, made circles beneath her shoulders. She moaned softly. "Brandt…"

"Yeah, beautiful?"

She laughed. "I can barely control myself." One hand slid down his back, found the immovable barrier of his leather belt. He kissed her softly and forced himself to separate their mouths.

"Don't worry, I'll take care of you," he said. But who was going to take care of him?

She stepped back from him, resting herself atop the bed, her blue eyes ablaze now, both lips trembling. He left the condoms on the nightstand and let his shirt fall to the floor. He watched her admire his body, felt his ego inflate a few degrees.

He sat on the edge of the mattress, denim rubbing against denim as their legs touched. His left hand locked along the side of her neck, his thumb rubbing across her jaw. He pulled her into a deep kiss, his tongue searching and probing inside her mouth. She moaned again, something that sounded like his name, and he made every effort to deepen the kiss, humming in response when her tongue flirted past his lips. Her hand ventured across his thigh, dangerously close to his core. He needed to be out of jeans, needed her naked beneath him. Again he cursed silently as he pulled their mouths apart, and set about removing her shirt. He unfastened the buttons with surprising adeptness, helping her out of the shirt, feeling the blazing skin beneath his hands as he did so.

He unfastened her bra, pushed one strap down and left a series of kisses along her collarbone and shoulder. He pulled her to the edge of the bed long enough for them to undress one another, his eyes sweeping the soft, sun-burnished surfaces of her skin, his mouth eager to venture past the places the sun couldn't touch. When she pushed his jeans to the floor and took him in hand, his guts twisted as he outwardly held himself together. Her naked flesh glancing his was nearly too much, and he placed her gently back atop the bed.

His attention returned to the nightstand. He felt like he was sixteen again, and it was his first time, his girlfriend's first time, and he'd gone fumble-fingered with the box. He set it down, took a deep breath, then picked it up and did what he had to do.

• • •

She watched his body, tall, lanky, and solid with muscle, slide between her legs. He sank deep into her, brought their hips together. She was as limp and relaxed as if she'd been drinking—and she was intoxicated, but not on spirits. Brandt propped on his elbows above her, pulsing as he burned inside.

"Do you feel okay?" he asked in a whisper.

"Perfect," she assured him. Which was exactly how their bodies fit together. This was a new experience, a man being so concerned with her comfort and not his own satisfaction. Her hand slipped into the V-shaped space formed by their bodies, her fingers following the arrow of dark hair from his navel upward. Her hand turned atop his heart, her palm and fingers tracing the hard lines of muscle and the soft, downy hair that looked almost golden in the lamplight. His eyes seemed to track the movement, his body shaking in response, their gazes locking as her hand found its way to his chin. He lay fully atop her then, her hands guiding his shoulders downward, her breasts pressed into the solid wall of his torso.

He moved slowly at first, gently against her, matching each touch of his lips to another thrust. She arched into him, heard the growl emanate somewhere deep in his chest as their hips matched in cadence. She pushed upward, asking for a quicker rhythm, her body eager to feel the downward slide of pressure, begging for the hardness to awaken her insides. "I love you," she heard him whisper, and she answered in harmony with his declaration. If their initial attraction had been bluntly physical, it had manifested itself into something sensitive and soulful—they were making love in its purest form.

His hand slid beneath her hip, then along her thigh, dragging her tighter to him as he increased the power of his strokes. Her release unfurled in waves, her body loosening and tightening as sensation washed through her. His own climax was seemingly endless as his body labored and shuddered against hers. She held him tightly as it gradually ceased, locking her body against his until the aftershocks slowed to a crawl and his chest stopped heaving. Two of their hands entwined, a smile forming as she stared into his sweaty, exhausted face. If the first time with him had been this good, what would the second time be like?

• • •

His lips hit the slick, salty skin of her abdomen. True, he tasted the combined heat and sweat of their two bodies, but he'd been eager to have his lips on her skin from day one. He wasn't going to complain, because she tasted great. He nibbled on her stomach, a fake bite, and she laughed in surprise.

"Aren't you tired?" she asked dreamily, her words lighter than air.

He laughed against her stomach. "Yeah, but I brought a whole box of insurance along, and I wasn't planning to leave here with it tonight."

"Proceed," she said, and he didn't have to be told twice. His body reverberated, long after their first encounter had resulted in a sweaty, earth-shattering climax. He'd never detonated quite like that before—an orgasm was always great, even better when the woman was someone you loved—but he'd never felt it grip him that fully, starting at the apex of his hips and racing through his body, across his skin, and meeting itself in a metaphorical figure eight. Even now the aftershocks hit him as he slid across her stomach. He took one breast in his mouth, found the peak already firm and unyielding against his tongue. One hand brushed his face, rubbing his ear until it burned. He moved to the other breast, delighted in the taste of her skin, the texture and color. Her body was smooth like a piece of a glass—and hot like glass that'd just been pulled from a kiln. Marissa bucked against him, a silent demand that he find his way back to her mouth.

Brandt was stubborn, though—always had been—and so his mouth lingered over her chest, brushed against her collarbone. "Beautiful," he murmured, and she sighed in happy resignation. Then she jumped in glad surprise as one hand found its way between them, fingertips parting her. His thumb slid upward, then down, reveling in the heat, the subtle tempo of her body as she moved against his hand. He pulled it away slowly, swiped at the nightstand, and sheathed himself inside her before he lost his nerve. She felt great the second time around, clenching him greedily, building rhythm a little too quickly. He slowed down, framed her face with his hands.

"This might sound a little trite, Marissa, but you are beautiful." He sank into her lips, felt them accept his mouth again and again. "And amazing. And wonderful." Each compliment was accompanied by another kiss, her tongue lavishing against his. "And too damned sexy for words."

"Then forget the words," she suggested, "and stick to this." Her hips locked him tight, her hands and arms held him against her, and he pushed deeper, again and again, until fire surged through him, left his body, and she twisted and wracked beneath him, their two bodies becoming replete yet unwilling to separate. When he was drained, but still trembling, he levered himself above Marissa, let his mouth kiss every inch of her face, his fingers brushing at the edges and pushing flaxen strands away from her ears and cheeks.

"I love you," he repeated. She lifted her head just enough to place a kiss along his shoulder…then his neck…then his face… and finally she smiled.

"I love you, Brandt Conner."

...

He pulled her atop him, and then alongside him—and then, when she was sure they'd both collapse from exhaustion, he rested atop her one last time and they made love slowly, the heat burning between them for what felt like an eternity until another release ripped their bodies apart.

In the aftermath, she figured Brandt had been saving up for a while, and she definitely had. She rested alongside him beneath the sheet, let her mouth enjoy one perfect, muscular arm, golden with a tan. His eyes were closed but he was still very much awake as her hand slid up the inside of his thigh. His body was as close to perfection as she'd ever seen, lines and sinews and muscles forming perfectly across his upper body; his hands, mouth, and lower body skillful at the art of pleasure. His shoulders were solid, and his stomach featured just the right amount of hair to brush against her belly, and send her mind spinning into madness. His face had been perfect from the moment they met, and at this point she found even his nose sexy. One thing, however, lingered on her mind.

"Brandt?" she asked, placing her mouth dangerously close to his left nipple.

"Hmm?" He perked up as her teeth brushed against him.

"Why do you walk with a limp?"

He chuckled. "Rodeo accident."

She draped one arm across his chest, and stared at him until those warm green eyes fluttered open. The smirk came to his mouth immediately. "Really," she retorted playfully. "My tongue is enjoying your body. The least you can do is be honest."

He shook his head against the pillow and laughed, a look on his face that was brand-new to her. Definitely an expression that rolled several happy sensations into one. She felt his chest rise and fall as he let out a deep breath. "When I was in high school, I broke my leg in a car accident. Fractured the femur clean in two." He grimaced as though the pain lingered, then gave her a tight smile. "The doctors said it healed up just fine, but I've favored it ever since the cast came off." His expression turned sheepish. "I hope that's not a disappointing end to the story. You noticed it straight off, didn't you?"

She nodded, her heart filling with love for him. "Nothing about you is a disappointment, Brandt." She rested her cheek atop his heart, pounding beneath the skin. "Nothing at all."

• • •

Brandt buttoned his shirt slowly, tucked in the tails, then sat down on the edge of the mattress to pull on his boots. Marissa sat alongside him, clad in a robe that ended above her knees. Perfect, sexy, gorgeous knees. Another place your mouth drifted, his mind recalled, and he smiled. "I'd stay the whole night," he apologized again. "I'm a big boy and my parents would only give it a brief thought." He rested his hands atop his thighs. "But Rawlings and I are already scheduled to move a few hundred pounds of feed and fertilizer tomorrow morning." He kissed her softly, then pulled his face back and smiled. "When you and I get married, you'll get used to it."

"'When'?" she echoed. He laughed at his slip of the tongue—but had it truly been a slip? He'd warmed considerably to the idea of marriage, even before he and Marissa spent a few heated hours together. Still, it was premature to consider a lifetime commitment. He was merely in the process of making this thing long-term.

"That's the problem with marrying a cowboy or a farmer," Brandt said, lifting her chin upward with one finger. "A lot of lonely hours." He kissed her again, on the cheek, the nose, and finally the mouth, a deep, intimate kiss. "But there's plenty of good points too."

"Oh?" she asked huskily.

"Yeah," he whispered. "Strong shoulders. He can carry you up the stairs…to bed…and keep you occupied until the rooster crows."

He felt two warm, sure hands envelop his neck, and Marissa pulled her face back to his. "You don't have to sell me on it, cowboy. So…"

He smiled at her brevity. "So…" Her fingers stirred enticingly at the back of his neck.

"We need to do this again sometime. Not just the physical side of things—which was great, by the way." He smiled proudly. "But the whole evening. I loved getting to know your family because it helped me understand you a little better."

He shrugged slightly. "I told you I was uncomplicated, beautiful."

"And I still don't quite believe you." Her thumb traced an outline of his mouth. "I have found you to be very kind, confident, and loyal." She pressed her lips against his pulse, warmth blanketing his neck in crimson. "It's that damned cologne," she said contritely. "Makes it hard for me to keep my hands off you."

He laughed again, the right corner of his mouth quirking up. "You sure it's got nothing to do with me? This face? This body?"

She smiled as she pulled him into one final kiss for the night. "Well, that might be part of it."

Chapter Ten

Brandt usually ate breakfast alone on Sunday mornings, his parents already at church as he scrambled eggs and made toast. It wasn't that he had a problem with organized religion, or God—he simply took the Sabbath as his one day of rest per week, where he didn't fling himself out of bed at the crack of dawn. Today he broke the pattern—he still buttered his toast in silence, but had no time for rest. He rapped gently at the door of the bunkhouse—Rawlings was awake but bleary-eyed as he shielded his face from the sun.

"Now this is a change," he joshed. "Usually I'm the first one in the barn every morning."

"The early bird gets the worm," was Brandt's simple reply. He didn't tell Rawlings he was well rested from a few hours of incredible, mind-blowing sex. He didn't have to, because the conversation would inevitably head in that direction. He'd just have to keep it clean, not show all his cards. Easier said than done, his conscience reminded him. They made their way inside the barn, and found Mitchell's truck situated halfway between the front and rear doors.

"How did things go last night?" Rawlings asked as he slung a fifty-pound bag of fertilizer over his shoulder like it was full of feathers. "How'd Mitch and Laura take to Marissa?"

Brandt gathered up a bag and smiled. The two men formed a pile of materials in the storage room that was reserved for this particular purpose. "I got home too late last night to do a follow-up, but they loved her during the meal. Mom was impressed immediately, and Dad came around about five seconds later."

"Sounds great," Rawlings said, straightening his gloves. Brandt grinned, and watched as the wheels clicked together inside his friend's head. Like clockwork, his mouth lifted into a smile of realization. "You got home late? Damn, man, you've been holding out on me."

Brandt shook his head. "I didn't really think it was my right to broadcast what happened, at least not in detail."

"Why don't you just give me the long and short of it?" Rawlings suggested.

"Interesting choice of words." He set down the bag he'd been holding and leaned against the tailgate. He folded both arms across his chest and flattened his lips into a contemplative line. "It's like when you build something up in your mind, and you keep pushing it higher until there's no way it can ever meet your expectations. Being with Marissa was like that, except it felt like nothing I've ever experienced." He summoned a memory from the previous night, a crystal-clear image of his face reflected in the sapphire blaze of her eyes just before they came together. "I can't tell you what happened because I can't put it into words."

Rawlings's reaction surprised him. "I want that, partner. I want to feel that kind of love with a woman before I grow old and die."

Brandt smiled enthusiastically. "You will, man. I promise." He slapped Rawlings on the shoulder. "Look, this was an accident, a twist of fate, something I certainly never planned for. Dad should've sent you after the fence that day, and Mom usually goes to pick out her own tomatoes. I'm damned glad those things got pushed off on me, though, because I need Marissa in my life."

"It never made sense before, did it?"

He was struck by Rawlings's insight, though he shouldn't have been. "No, it didn't. When I get that tightness in my gut now, I know it's because I want to be with her—not because I can't figure out why we're together."

"She's got you roped and tied."

Brandt laughed. "Definitely." He made a motion with his head and they resumed their work, not talking much. Some things didn't need to be expressed between them; some words could be understood without ever being spoken. When the truck bed was empty, they climbed inside and Brandt turned over the engine, driving out the back doors of the barn and heading across the ranch. They rolled down the windows, letting the clean, fresh spring air filter inside as they made a slow circuit of the land. The place was greening back to life, flowering trees replacing their blooms with leaves; the grass was no longer dormant, its blades headed skyward, or more likely toward the mouth of a cow. Squirrels bounced up trees, knocking bark to the ground in the process, and rabbits scurried to the safety of their holes.

"I just realized what we forgot to add to the list," Rawlings announced.

Brandt tapped his fingers against the steering wheel—with the truck moving no more than five miles per hour, he drove with his thumbs. "What's that?" he asked.

"Chicken feed."

"Shit," Brandt answered. "I'm ready to kill that rooster on a good day, but starvation ain't the way to do it."

Rawlings rested one arm along the open windowsill of the truck door. "You know what this means, don't you?"

"What might that be, Rawlings?"

"You're gonna hate it."

"Try me."

"Well," he said, turning his head toward his friend, "you've gotta hit the farm store first thing in the morning."

Brandt responded with a closed-mouth grin. "Hmm. You're right, it sounds like torture."

•••

With much of Layton still at church, the restaurant was nearly empty for brunch. Sunlight cascaded past rows of tall windows, blanketing exposed brick walls with golden rays. Local artwork dotted the walls here and there, and the sound of clanking dishes and silverware filled the atmosphere. Rowan picked through her strawberry salad as she spoke. "How did everything go last night?"

Marissa popped a grape into her mouth and smiled. "Wonderfully. Brandt's parents are great—it's easy to see where his good looks came from. His dad is friendly but a little standoffish. He and Brandt have a tense relationship, but they put on a good show for me. And his mother is just plain sweet, kind, and generous. She radiates warmth as soon as she enters a room."

Rowan nodded as she chewed. "An instant rapport with the parents is definitely a good thing."

"The evening only got better from there," Marissa said absently as she finished her fruit salad. Rowan stopped eating and glanced across the table. "Without revealing too much," she continued, "I'll just tell you that it was very, very hard to let him go home afterward."

"I guess that explains why you haven't stopped smiling all morning. You got in my car with that grin plastered to your face, and it hasn't let up since."

"Really?" Marissa asked. "I hadn't noticed," she joked, as she noted the increasing upward curvature of her mouth. "That reminds me," she said, snapping to attention. Rowan glanced at her expectantly. "In the midst of…other things…Brandt and I talked about Wednesday night for our double date. How does that sound?"

Rowan smiled. "Works for me. But will the two of you be able to keep your hands off one another long enough to go on a date?"

Marissa pondered it for a few seconds, her eyes glancing over to the door, where customers were filtering through at an increased rate. "That remains to be seen—but I promise we'll try our best."

● ● ●

Brandt's parents ate lunch in town after church, but he still had dishes to do. He was halfway up to his elbows in sudsy water when Laura walked into the kitchen, having replaced her Sunday best with jeans, her long hair now pinned up for comfort.

"How was the sermon this morning?" he asked, his back toward her. She quickly settled into place alongside him, watching in reserve as he rinsed dishes and set them in the drainer.

"Mercifully short," she answered, and Brandt couldn't help but laugh. Laura was the kindest person he knew, but she had little patience for long, meandering sermons with no purpose. "The Bible is perfect as-is," she'd once told him. "No need for extra embellishments when a simple psalm will do." He smiled to himself, wondering if her advice had anything to do with the conciseness of his own speech pattern. "Your father and I ran into Marissa on our way to lunch."

"Oh?"

"She was with a pretty red-haired girl."

"That's Rowan," Brandt explained. "Rawlings's future girlfriend, if we have anything to say about it."

Laura nodded. "She was very lovely. I'm sure he'll be pleased to meet her."

"Hope so."

There was a lull in the conversation as Brandt placed a skillet underwater to soak. Their eyes met just long enough for him to absorb that there was something important on her mind.

"You've only just met Marissa, but I can sense that the two of you are very serious. Am I wrong?"

He smiled briefly as his hands returned to the water. "No, you're not wrong. I didn't expect it, but I'm pretty sure this is the girl I want to marry."

"How sure?" she prompted gently.

"About a hundred percent," he responded briskly.

She replied with a laugh and patted him on the shoulder. "You know, when I married your father, I was only about ninety percent sure it was the right thing to do."

Brandt stifled his own laugh—barely. Laura smiled at him. "Any regrets?"

"None," she said. "I haven't regretted a day of our lives together." She paused for what Brandt figured was a moment of reflection. "You know that the secret to marriage is compromise."

He met her eyes and nodded. "I think that's the secret to life on the whole, Mom."

She smiled warmly. "It's also about not expecting your partner to be perfect, but expecting to always love them."

"Sounds like pretty good advice."

"I hope so."

With the dishes completed, Brandt let the water out of the sink and dried his hands. He turned and leaned against the counter, crossing his arms across his chest. "I'd like to spend as much time as I possibly can with her, but I know that's unrealistic."

His mother nodded sympathetically. "She has to work, and so do you. Welcome to the real world, son."

He groaned, and tried for a frown that didn't take. He wound up smiling, and enjoying his mother's words of wisdom. "I'll try to get her to come out here on the weekend. I'm sure you could use the female companionship."

"Not that I don't enjoy you and your father and young Mr. McCoy, but yes, that would be welcome."

"And now I've invaded your only sanctuary, otherwise known as the kitchen."

She laughed at his gentle teasing. "Believe me, Marissa will never complain if you offer to cook dinner."

"So noted. By the way, has Dad ever cooked for you?"

Laura puzzled on it before answering. "I think so, although not in this century. I'll get back to you on that one."

Brandt leaned down and kissed her on the forehead. "You're the best, Mom. I'm gonna do a little target practice with Rawlings, okay?"

"Be safe," she said. "Take your earplugs."

"Already in my pocket."

"Have fun."

He turned on his heel and winked at her before heading through the door. "Always."

...

"What do we think about this shirt?" Rowan held it aloft, across her chest like she was some kind of model. "Too garish?"

Marissa scrunched up her nose and laughed. The button-down consisted of wide pink and purple vertical stripes with white scrollwork embroidered through the fabric—it looked more like a circus tent than first-date material. "That's one way of putting it. Listen, I promise that Rawlings will think you're gorgeous no matter what you wear."

Rowan returned the shirt to its rack and nodded. "It's been entirely too long since a man looked at me with love in his eyes, so you might call me a little gun-shy."

"I was in a major drought when Brandt showed up," Marissa reminded her. "And I still made him wait." They made their way through the store, past the clearance racks and off-season shoes priced to move. "Which, now that I think about it, was not such a bad idea." She studied Rowan's face. "I'm not boring you, am I?"

"Absolutely not," she replied. "Believe me, most of my time is spent with teenagers, who are even more conceited and vapid than when we were at their age."

"Hard to imagine."

"So any conversation I get to have with an adult, and any encounter with a grown man, are more than welcome." She pulled a light-green Western shirt from the front of the rack and held it up. "How about this?"

Marissa nodded. "That's the one—it brings out the color of your eyes." Rowan folded it across her arm and they headed toward the shoe section. "That reminds me—I spoke to my mother this morning."

"Did you talk to her about Brandt?"

"Some. She wants to know if we've set a date, of course."

"Ha-ha," Rowan said drily. "It's not a bad idea, but a little premature."

"She just wants me to be happy. Even though she and my father split up when I was young, she's never tried to dissuade me from the idea of lasting happiness, of finding love with the right man."

Rowan angled her head to one side. "Can't give up hope, can we?"

Marissa laughed. "No, because sometimes hope is all we have left."

"How should I wear my hair?"

"Honestly?" Marissa looked at her with a frown. "I would just wear it down. You've got enough natural wave and curl to not have to bother with it."

"Great for a first date, not so much when the humidity kicks up."

"See, I'm totally looking forward to summer."

Rowan grinned at her. "I'm pretty sure I have a good idea why, but fill in the blanks—help your friend out."

"What else? I'm pretty sure Brandt will start running around shirtless."

"You really have it bad, don't you?"

Marissa nodded. "Uh-huh. And with any luck, you'll catch this disease too."

Chapter Eleven

"It's always nerve-wracking to meet the parents, huh?" Josie asked at a whisper. She and Marissa stood behind the counter, unwrapping small items and placing them in the glass case. So far Marissa had granted a few precious details, more or less keeping the best parts of Saturday evening to herself. What she and Brandt had shared not only was no one else's business, but also far too intimate to ever be expressed in words.

"It was," Marissa confirmed, "but my fears were quickly put to rest, and the entire evening was amazing." She arranged a series of pocketknives, checked it from every angle, and locked the case up tight.

"I'm pretty desperate for romance," Josie admitted, "so kudos to you for finding some."

"Don't worry," Marissa answered with a smile. "It'll come in its own time." They continued with their chitchat, letting it fall away when they heard Mona's footsteps clicking against the wooden floor. Mona studied them for several frightening moments before she offered to speak.

"Josie, I'd like your help in the storeroom today. Go on back there and I'll join you in a few minutes." When she'd left, Mona turned her attention to Marissa. "I'd like you to mind the register—if anyone needs assistance outdoors, page me."

"I can do that," Marissa answered. Her shoulders tightened with anxiety—was Mona about to give her some sort of dressing-down? She'd been a dedicated employee, punctual and helpful, cleaning the store without even being prompted. Or was it something even worse, something Brandt-centered?

"I must admit I've been a little concerned about you," Mona said, clearly shooting for worry but failing miserably. "Moving to a new town can be tough—believe me, I know." Marissa nodded—sometimes she forgot that Mona, as an old friend of her mother's, wasn't from Layton, either. "I've wondered if you were able to make friends, and I remembered that you and Britt were around the same age. I'm sure she'd be willing to introduce you to others in your age group."

Marissa smiled as she hurried to compose a response that wouldn't sound a) condescending or b) rude. And "Hell no" wouldn't work in this situation, either. Britt was the absolute last person she wanted as a friend. She already knew too much about Mona's allegedly perfect daughter. "Thank you, Mona, but that's not necessary. Josie is a good friend here at the store, and I have another friend from high school who just happens to live in Layton."

"That's good," Mona answered, obviously chastened. "Any romantic prospects?"

"I'm still settling in, finding my bearings," Marissa lied. "I'm just not interested in all of that right now."

Mona seemed satisfied by that answer, and was ready to head to the storeroom when her eyes locked onto the glass door at the front of the building. "Here comes trouble," she said, disdain evident in her tone. Marissa followed her gaze, and her eyes widened when Brandt pushed through the front door in his familiar shuffle, one leg not quite as graceful as the other.

Not that any of that had mattered in bed.

She felt herself redden with distress—or something more carnal—but as Brandt stopped directly in front of her, his expression remained neutral, the burn in his green eyes kept below a simmer.

"Mona," he said, acknowledging her with a tip of his hat.

"Brandt," she answered without inflection. "I spoke to your mother after church yesterday. She said you'd been keeping busy with the ranch."

"That's right." Marissa noted the level tone in his voice, and when his gaze swung around to her, there was the hint of a smirk on his lips. "Miss Sloan, I need four bags of chicken feed."

"Large or small?"

"Large," he said, drawling out the word. She kept her expression impassive, but inside her head every manner of off-color comments bounced amongst the synapses. "Hopefully my dad won't be too upset that I forgot to pick them up last week."

Marissa picked up the laminated sheet of paper that contained the barcodes for the fertilizer and feed, scanned the appropriate one, and multiplied it by four on the register. She gave the amount and Brandt's fingers brushed hers intentionally as money changed hands. Interesting, she thought, but not unfortunate that he declined to use his father's line of credit that particular day. "You know where the feed is," she said.

He nodded as he pocketed the change. "Sure do. Have a nice day, ma'am." He tipped down brim of his hat, gave Marissa the briefest of winks. "Mona," he said over his shoulder as he headed for the door.

She answered quickly, "Good day, Brandt," her mouth set into the kind of firm line a manager should never use with a paying customer.

"Thank you, and come again," Marissa said, blanching at her words briefly before composing herself. She smiled as Brandt exited the store, and she watched him haul the bags—easily—from their shed outside to his truck. When he climbed inside the truck, their eyes met for the most fleeting of moments through two layers of glass, and then he shifted into reverse and drove away.

"He leered at you last time," Mona said, not bothering to hide her disgust. "He was far more of a gentleman this time. He almost fooled me, which is not easily done." She shook her head. "I'll be back to check on you in a bit, Marissa. Keep up the good work."

Marissa watched her return to the back of the store, one eyebrow raised in cheerful insubordination. Brandt didn't have to leer this time, she thought to herself with a huge grin. I've got nothing to hide from him. And when her phone buzzed in her pocket a half-hour later, as she was ringing up another customer, she didn't have to bother checking it. She already knew what it would say.

• • •

Brandt kissed the curve where her neck and shoulder came together, tracked his lips across the warm expanse of skin, the surface tingling against his mouth. He lifted his head and glanced at her beautiful face in profile. Her eyes were closed, but she wasn't quite dozing. He left one kiss atop her cheek and smiled as her mouth turned upward.

"Didn't we have a date scheduled for tonight?" she asked.

He laughed. "I thought we'd get this out of the way first." His lips hit the corner of her mouth. "Have I ever told you how sexy you are?"

"Not in the last five minutes," she said, and they both laughed. She nestled into his stomach and he swallowed hard—every time their skin touched, no matter how briefly, it sent electricity coursing through his body. He lifted his thumb and wiped a bead of sweat away from her hairline.

"If you keep doing that," he warned, her thighs teasing him, "we're never going to make it to dinner."

"Hmm," she replied. His fingertips slid down her chest, and she hummed in response. "Do you think my breasts are too small?"

His thumb slid around one nipple. "I think they're perfect." He kissed her earlobe. "Where did that question come from?"

"I don't know," she hedged, her stomach undulating beneath his fingers. He splayed them across the surface, pulling her still closer to him. "Don't men fixate on that kind of thing?"

"Only if they've never seen a pair before."

He heard her sigh in response. "Seriously?"

"Would I lie to you?" When she didn't answer immediately, he added, "A man who truly loves you, loves you for the person inside. Sure, great packaging helps, but beauty is only skin deep. In your case, every part of you is beautiful. You know what part of you I really, really enjoy?"

"Uh-uh."

He pushed the sheet away from her body, pointed his fingers south across her abdomen. "I like this tan line right here." His eyes ventured where the skin turned lighter just below her navel. "There's a nice borderline between what the rest of the world gets to see—and what only I get to see."

"Brute," she murmured, a second before she chased it with laughter.

"Would a brute do this?" he asked, dipping his fingers inside her. She jumped in pleasant surprise.

"Absolutely," she responded distantly, as he hardened against her. When he united their bodies once again, they both came in a matter of seconds.

"We're going to dinner tonight, I promise," he said, gasping for breath as he kissed her forehead. He smiled when he felt her hands framing his face.

"At this point," she said, "I don't have the energy to do anything *but* eat."

•••

"I won't be here, so I'm counting on you to sign for the deliveries that day. Any questions?"

Marissa nodded, and did her best to listen to Mona's directives, but to no avail. Every available square inch of her mind had been given over to Brandt—his mouth, his hands, his body, and the way he seemed to use all of them in concert. Her thoughts weren't purely lustful, though. She thought too, about his inherent ability to say exactly what she needed to hear at any given time. He never seemed to run out of adjectives to describe how smart and beautiful she was. If this was the steamiest relationship she'd ever been in, it was also the most mature. Even though he preferred not to, Brandt could easily carry on a conversation about everything from art history to firearms.

"Would you like me to stay late and lock up?" she finally offered when Mona had come to a pause in the conversation. "I know sometimes there are deliveries after closing time."

Mona smiled in gratitude. "That would be very helpful. Thank you, Marissa."

They both turned toward the door as a deliveryman pushed through, holding a rectangular vase full of red tulips, their blooms perfectly clumped together in a square formation. His bright smile cut through the dim, wooden-clad surroundings of the store. The windows, Marissa thought ruefully, admitted a great amount of light, rays of sun that were all too quickly sucked up by the store's interior. It really was time for Mona or her husband to repaint the whole place—white would be a good start, or even a pale blue. "I have a delivery here for Marissa Sloan," he said cheerfully.

"That would be me," Marissa said, swallowing nervously. Surely Brandt wouldn't do this? Would he?

He sat the vase carefully atop the counter and handed her a receipt that she quickly signed. "Beautiful arrangement," he said. "Have a nice day," he added, smiling as he turned to leave.

"Thank you," Marissa said absently, her attention turning to the card.

"I thought you said you had no time for romance?" Mona inquired, one eyebrow slightly arched.

Marissa reached for the card, opening the envelope with all the care a snake charmer might use to coax one of their pets to perform. When she read the card, she stifled a laugh—and another urge, deep inside her body.

"What does it say?" Mona asked nosily. Marissa handed her the card and her brows furrowed in confusion. "Borderline? What kind of message is that?"

"It's from my mother," Marissa fibbed, her voice coming out with a slight rasp. "It's been an inside joke ever since I moved across the border. She's glad I'm doing well, but she still misses me."

"That was very sweet of Connie," Mona said. "Thanks again for your help."

"You're welcome," Marissa said, her eyes darting once again to the flowers. Brandt definitely understood romance. She grabbed her phone from its pocket, and tapped in a message: "Nice flowers—you are so getting lucky the next time we're alone."

His reply came soon after, concise and to the point, and it was very easy for her to imagine the roguish smile on his face as he tapped it out: "Wouldn't I have anyway?"

She laughed softly, put her phone away, and smiled as she stared out the windows. "Yeah," she said to herself. "You probably would have."

• • •

"I'm as nervous as a whore in church."

Brandt laughed out loud, and would've laughed even harder had he not been driving. Rawlings was in the passenger seat, throwing out bizarre quips left and right, his hands knotted together like a piece of rope.

"Okay," Brandt advised, his stomach still shaking with residual laughter, "that's exactly the kind of thing you shouldn't say at dinner. I've met Rowan once or twice and she's a great girl. You're going to get along like turkey and gravy." They stopped at a red light, and Rawlings gave him an open-mouthed look of disbelief. "What?"

"I can't talk about whores in church, but you can throw out metaphors about turkey? Lame, bud, lame."

Brandt lifted one hand in defeat as he hit the accelerator. "It's the best I can do at the moment. Besides, you're worried for nothing. Marissa and I will both be there the whole time, to stimulate conversation." At the word "stimulate," something flashed through his mind, and he was forced to push it aside. "It's all gonna work out fine."

"Brandt…"

"Hmm?"

"Your optimism is killing me."

He laughed out loud again, the sound echoing through the truck's interior. "I won't let you die, I promise—at least not until I see you happy." He had a moment of clarity, and spared his friend a helpful glance. "And, Rawlings?"

"Yeah?" he asked, his face awash in curiosity.

"Take off your hat when you meet Rowan. Let her see that pretty, dark hair of yours." Rawlings shot him a surly glance, but as Brandt returned his attention to the road, he watched his friend out of the corner of his eye, saw him remove his hat long enough to make a few sweeps through his coffee-colored locks with his fingers. Brandt laughed silently to himself.

• • •

"Are they here yet?"

Marissa laughed and glanced toward her friend. "Not yet, Rowan. I'll let you know." They were already parked outside the restaurant, the windows rolled down. "Look at it like this," she'd told Brandt earlier. "If the date is lousy, they can drink away their sorrows." A nice breeze floated through the car, any residual heat from the day being tamped down as the evening wore on. "Brandt's truck is black," she reiterated. "He's kind of stealthy."

Rowan drummed her fingertips on the console. "How do I look?"

"With your eyes," Marissa teased, and smiled as her friend replied with a frown. "You look great, I promise." Rowan was dressed in the green shirt from the shopping trip, jeans, and boots, and her long, red hair had been flat-ironed until it was straight. It wasn't what they'd discussed, but the overall effect was very nice. She only hoped Rawlings would be impressed.

"Maybe this wasn't the best idea," Rowan fretted. Marissa placed a hand along her forearm, firmly, and their eyes met.

"This was your idea, remember? You begged me for details about Brandt, and whether or not he had a friend. You were intrigued the second you saw his picture. Everything is going to be fine. Rawlings is a great guy. Come on—would I steer you wrong?"

She watched Rowan's face lose its tension. "No, you wouldn't. You really have been an amazing friend lately."

"Same here. Making friends has never been my strong suit," Marissa admitted. "Thank God for putting Layton in my path." Her smile broadened as she saw Brandt wheel into the parking lot, then pull to a stop alongside them. "Our men have arrived."

"Oh, God," Rowan said, checking her makeup in the rearview mirror. "How is my hair?"

"Just relax," Marissa advised her. "You spend your days with teenagers—you can handle anything."

Brandt stepped out of the driver's side, looking dashing as usual as he snapped his hat atop his head. Rawlings followed, a few steps behind, and adjusted the brim of his own hat before he yanked it off and held it nervously in one hand while he used the other to straighten his hair.

"Rowan Altman, this is Rawlings McCoy," Brandt said in his purely masculine, authoritative drawl. They shook hands and Marissa watched, transfixed, as sparks flew through the air. It didn't seem possible, but lightning appeared to have struck yet again.

"Nice to meet you," Rawlings said, his hand unable to relinquish his date's.

"The pleasure is all mine," Rowan answered. Their eyes were locked together like heat-seeking missiles on target. Marissa didn't notice that Brandt had put his arm around her shoulder until she felt his lips against her earlobe.

"Looks like you did a good job," he whispered. "Those two appear to be hitting it off."

"What can I say? I'm a natural at this love thing."

"Is that so?" he asked, his breath hot as fire against her cheek.

"Oh, yeah," she answered, nestling against his shoulder. "After all, I said yes to you."

He laughed, then pulled away in order to raise his voice. "Okay, kids, time for dinner. And no complaints when I tell you it's on me."

"Which means we're getting the cheapest items on the menu," Rawlings warned them. "Mr. Conner is a cheapskate of the highest order."

"Hey, I resent that remark," Brandt said. He held the door for each of them and they strolled into the air-conditioned, country music soundtracked restaurant. He slipped one hand around Marissa's waist. "They're playing our song, Miss Sloan."

"Later, cowboy," she answered teasingly. "Our nest isn't empty tonight."

"Damn," he said with a smile in his voice. They slid into the booth, both men seated together on one side, facing the women.

The waitress took their drink orders and they pored over the menus. "So, Rowan," Brandt said, "you wouldn't know it to look at this guy, but he's actually a pretty good hand in the kitchen."

"I don't know whether to take that as a compliment or an insult," Rawlings said with a grin.

"My cooking skills are rudimentary at best," Rowan said. "But I'm learning."

"You'll have to come with me to Brandt's house sometime," Marissa suggested. "His mother is an amazing cook."

"I'd like that," she replied.

"The ranch is beautiful this time of year," Rawlings said uneasily. Brandt elbowed him to continue, and when Marissa met his eyes, she saw a measure of pride in them. "It's actually beautiful anytime, but right now the flowering trees are in bloom, some of them have already leafed out…"

"It helps if you don't mind cow manure," Brandt joked.

"When you're a school teacher," Rowan assured them, "you learn how to deal with bullshit."

They all laughed. "And I sell plenty of shit at the store," Marissa pointed out. "See? We're all kindred spirits."

Food was ordered, and more than a few bottles of beer were consumed. Stories were swapped about the good old days in both Layton and Brackville, anecdotes from the days before their lives became complicated, filled with time clocks, bills, strife, and the idiosyncrasies that came with the passage of time.

"You know the old adage, 'beer then liquor, never sicker'?" Brandt said. Rowan nodded. "Rawlings and I set out to prove that wrong, and at seventeen years old we were just arrogant enough to think we could pull it off." Brandt tossed a potato wedge in his mouth and chased it with some beer. He rubbed condensation from his bottle and smiled at the memory. Marissa was enjoying hearing some of these stories again—they were just as funny the second time around.

"And we just about succeeded," Rawlings said, wincing, "but I challenged Brandt to finish that bottle of Jim Beam. Big mistake."

Brandt shook his head in disgust. "Have you ever seen two full-grown men retch until their stomachs were sore? Not a pretty sight."

"What'd your parents say?" Rowan asked.

"My dad laughed his head off," Brandt said, "which is not the sound you're anxious to hear when you're hungover."

"What about Laura?" Marissa asked. "I bet she had an equally-livid reaction."

"When we'd finished sobering up," Rawlings said, "Brandt's mom sent us up to the attic. You ever tried to clean the attic of an old farmhouse? You'd just as soon straighten up a landfill as deal with that mess."

"It wasn't all bad, though," Brandt recalled. "Some of that old crap wound up being valuable, at least to people driving down the highway. We made a lot of money at that yard sale. Enough to buy another bottle of Jim."

"You'll notice all of their stories involve alcohol in some shape or form," Marissa observed drily.

Rowan shrugged. "Boys will be boys."

Dinner was over all too quickly, Marissa thought, but the evening had been a fun one—Brandt and Rawlings had no shortage of stories, and she and Rowan had contributed a few as well, though theirs were all sober ones. Outside the restaurant Brandt whispered a request in her ear, and even without the passionate kiss that followed, she was more than happy to indulge him.

•••

"I thought this was your secret spot?"

Brandt had one arm draped over Marissa's shoulder, his fingertips dangling perilously close to her breast. It was tempting, to be sure, to reach down and brush the peak, feel it rise through the fabric, but they had an audience. Their feet hung from the tailgate, where they were perched, as he watched Rawlings coax Rowan into the shallow creek. Their boots lay together in the grass at the shoreline, and he held her hand as they tiptoed barefoot through the chilled spring water. The shadows of sunset surrounded them, sending orange and blue streaks across the clear surface of the stream. Brandt gave a slight shrug in dereference to Marissa's inquiry. "What kind of wingman would I be if I didn't drag my buddy and his date to the most romantic spot I know?"

She ran one hand up this thigh—now she was the one getting dangerously close—and rested her head against him. "Yet another reason that I fell in love with you, Brandt. You always go the extra mile."

Rawlings dipped a hand in the water, whipped it out, and splashed a few droplets onto Rowan's jeans. She laughed, and he grinned like a kid the whole time. Brandt smiled—it'd definitely been a while since he'd seen his friend so happy, so carefree. Maybe, he thought, there'd be plenty more days like this—for each of them.

He angled his head just enough to catch the golden reflection of sunlight in Marissa's eyes. It made something catch in his heart, something he hadn't expected. The words came forth before he could overthink them, or consider something different. "I love you, Marissa. Always."

Chapter Twelve

Brandt stared at himself in the mirror as he refastened the buttons on his shirt. The red flush was slowly disappearing from his torso, but his veins were still thrumming with the after-effects. Marissa stood alongside him, brushing out the hair he'd spent the previous half-hour plaiting with his fingers, until it'd been completely disheveled and scattered across the pillow. This was becoming a good—or bad—habit, depending on one's perspective: showing up at Marissa's apartment for a date, only to wind up falling into her bed. He'd teased her earlier about being a fly tangled up in her spider's web, and she'd locked her hips that much tighter around him. It was a good memory, and made him hungry for more. But food was his paramount concern at this moment. After all, he'd promised the lady an evening out.

"We did a pretty good acting job the other day, you and me."

Marissa looked at him and smiled, her blue eyes still limpid and sated. "Only a trained professional—which Mona clearly isn't—would've spotted the signs." She laid the brush aside and grabbed a hair clasp. "But you nearly ruined it with the flowers. Thankfully you had the good sense not to sign the card."

He laughed. "If I can help it, I'll try to keep you from getting in trouble with the boss lady. When I was downtown, I saw that arrangement in the window at the flower shop and couldn't resist."

"Believe me," she said, another cute smiling forming, "they were more than appreciated—which you just discovered for yourself."

"Twice," he recalled with a self-satisfied grin.

"Uh-huh." He tucked in his shirttails and was checking his buttons one last time when she added, "Give me a kiss before I reapply my lipstick."

"Yes, ma'am," he drawled softly, pulling her into the circle formed by his arms. Her tongue searched the inside of his mouth, and he felt the warmth of her touch sliding through his veins yet again.

When they separated, she looked up at him in what he could only peg as admiration. "You're kind of sweet, you know that?"

"Don't tell anyone," he joked. "I've got a reputation to maintain."

"Your secret is safe with me." She patted him on the chest. "Now, give a girl a few minutes of privacy."

He saw her smirk, laughed, and went to park himself on the couch in her living room. He rested his right ankle across his left knee after he'd sat down, and grabbed his boot with one hand in what he recognized as a nervous tic. He scanned the interior of Marissa's apartment—she was a self-professed neat freak, and he'd never seen the place anything less than tidy. His eyes gradually made their way to the coffee table, where he spotted a glossy picture book of covered bridges, and a thinner booklet beneath it. He frowned and reached for it before withdrawing his hand…then he reached for it again. It was a college pamphlet, the kind that listed various programs and social activities. He recognized it—it was from the same university where he'd earned his four-year degree. He picked it up and thumbed through the pages. The campus had changed a little bit in the three years since he graduated—new restaurants, new housing, a new baseball diamond.

"Brandt?"

He looked up at her, took note of the anxiety etched into her features. The smiling eyes he'd left just a few minutes earlier— hell, he'd put that smile in them—were now turned down along with her mouth. "I'm sorry, sweetheart," he said, holding the book aloft. "I know it wasn't my place to look at your stuff."

"It's not that," she said, shaking her head. "As far as I'm concerned, nothing is off-limits. I have nothing to hide." She tilted her head toward his hand, which held the booklet limply. "Except maybe that."

He laid the book atop the table once again, regretting that he'd picked it up in the first place. She found a place beside him on the couch, bending her leg at the knee so her shinbone was against his thigh. "Do you wanna talk about it?" he asked worriedly. "If you don't, I won't force you."

Her smile was fragile now, but still beautiful. She exhaled, took in a deep breath, and opened her mouth to speak. "You know I wanted to be a therapist when I was growing up?" He nodded in remembrance. "Rowan suggested I take a circuitous route, try to get a degree in counseling. Maybe I could get a job at one of the schools around here. I requested the information from the school, partly because it's your alma mater but also because it's a good program. I could take some courses this summer online in an effort to boost my GPA, maybe start the program as early as this fall. More likely it would be next spring." He kept his gaze firmly on hers, finding yet again that the Marissa behind the blue eyes was even more beautiful than the woman he saw on the outside. It damned near took his breath away, the realization of that. "It's easy to get a degree online these days—I could get my Master's without ever stepping foot in a classroom—but I'm not sure I want that. I want to apply for internships and assistantships and work hands-on with kids and immerse myself in it. If I'm admitted, that is. It's a long shot, but maybe with a few extra years' worth of life experience, I'd make a better candidate." Marissa sighed. "The university is about a hundred miles away, though."

Seventy-five, but who's counting, Brandt thought silently.

Brandt took her right hand in his left, placed his other hand atop her knee. He squeezed both reassuringly. "You are, without a doubt, the smartest person I've ever met. Any program would be foolish not to take you, and the ones that didn't admit you before clearly didn't deserve you. Apply, sweetheart. Get those letters of recommendation and polish up that essay." She smiled, and he saw a tear leak from the corner of her eye—a happy tear. "Have I ever told you how amazing you are?"

"What does this mean for us, Brandt? For our future? I know we just started dating, but I really want to be with you. Really, really want to be with you."

He figured as much—the imprint of her lips was probably still somewhere on his chest. "We'll work it out," he said unconvincingly. Then he squared his shoulders and pulled her into a deep, needful kiss. He'd lost women to other men, or because they just weren't right together, but he'd never lost one to college. He couldn't keep her from her dream, but he couldn't figure a way around it, either. Nothing rash came to mind, but neither did a clear-cut solution to this brand-new problem. She felt so right in his arms, moaning softly against his chest—he just wished he had all the answers.

Then again, who didn't?

• • •

"Penny for your thoughts?"

Brandt smiled at her and tapped his fingers against the palm of her hand as it lay upright on the table. He'd remained stoic throughout dinner, but she knew her earlier admission must've thrown him for a loop. What to do, she wondered. A few short weeks ago she'd been new in town, worried about nothing more than a paycheck. Now she was in love, and getting a second chance to pursue her education. Sure, it wouldn't be easy—money would be an issue—but she'd never seen herself as a quitter and she didn't plan to start now.

Brandt stood not in the way of her happiness, but somewhere to the side. Could she have both—her education and her handsome, tender, amazing cowboy? It didn't seem a fair choice to make—but then again, when was life ever fair?

He gave her a crooked smile. "I was just thinking about how you and I got rejected for the second date. Our companionship was not solicited."

Marissa laughed—she knew of what he spoke. Rawlings had asked Rowan out on a second date, just the two of them, and she'd accepted before he was even finished with the question. Marissa had known it was inevitable, but she also felt a pang of responsibility. She didn't want them leaving the nest before they were ready. "Looks like those two are going to work out."

Brandt nodded. "He couldn't stop talking about her the whole way home. 'Brandt, did you see how hot she was?'" He laughed. "I had to remind him my heart was already spoken for. But I was glad to see McCoy so happy. Honestly."

"I believe you," she said.

"He's not had it easy."

"I know."

He must've caught something in her tone, because his eyebrows lifted. "About what happened earlier, Marissa. I don't have all the answers, but *when* you get accepted," he said, emphasizing the word, "I'm not letting you go."

"What?" she asked, suddenly taken aback.

He laughed in a self-deprecating manner. "I really screwed that one up, beautiful. I meant to say that I'd find some way to make the long-distance thing work. I won't stand in the way of your dreams."

"What if we're not strong enough?" she asked. He rubbed his thumb in a circular motion across her palm. "This is still new."

He shook his head in reply. "I'm smart enough to know a good thing when I find it." She met his gaze and, as usual, she found a lot of understanding there in his green eyes. "We've also got the rest of spring and the whole summer to spend together."

"You've got the ranch, and I've got work," she reminded him. "Our lives are pretty hectic sometimes."

"No one ever said life was easy," he pronounced, "unless you've got a trust fund. Anyway, once you're more educated than I am, I'm liable to develop an inferiority complex." There was a twinkle in his eyes now. "And I'll need you around in order to prove my manhood."

She laughed at the grin that formed quickly on his lips, and then he joined her. There was a little too much tension in the air tonight, a little too much concern over something that, given her past luck, was unlikely to happen anyway. "From what I've seen—and felt—thus far, your manhood seems built for the long-haul. I do look forward, however, to seeing where things go for us. I'm happier than I've ever been in my life."

"Same here," he admitted easily. "You're spoiling me."

She shot him an amused look. "Am I now?"

"Yeah," he said, dipping his chin toward the table. "Surely I don't deserve to be with such a beautiful woman?"

"Brandt Conner," she said, "when you cross the street, women rubberneck at dangerous levels."

"So that's what caused that pileup on Main Street the other day…" he replied, a wicked grin touching his mouth.

"I should have known you were teasing me," she retorted, "because humility isn't your style."

"I let my good looks do the talking for me."

"Mm-hmm," she said. "I'll punish you for that later."

"Kick me out of bed?" he asked worriedly.

"No," she said, and watched his face lift. "Never."

He became subdued on the drive home, and when he walked her to the door his kiss was no less potent, but he turned down her offer to come inside. "I'm expected in the garden early tomorrow morning. When should we get together again?"

"I'll probably be tired after work tomorrow, since I'm closing. Saturday?"

"Sounds great," he said, saying goodbye with one last kiss. From the safety of her apartment, she watched him drive away, his taillights vanishing in the darkness. She sighed, then flopped down onto the couch. The college brochure still lay on the coffee table, taunting her. She picked it up and flipped through the pages.

"You caused me a whole lot of trouble tonight," she said to the booklet, "but at least the cat's out of the bag. Time to work on that admissions essay—if nothing else, it'll help me sleep better tonight."

• • •

Brandt had been busy with his own series of projects, and Rawlings the same, so they didn't get a chance to confer prior to Rawlings and Rowan's date Friday night. When Brandt knocked on the front door of the bunkhouse Saturday morning for both a progress report and some friendly advice, he was startled to receive no answer. He cupped one hand against the window, but no light spilled through the curtains. He worried for a minute—either something bad had happened, or Rawlings was sleeping like the dead.

"Brandt," he heard his father's voice call out. Mitchell must've heard him banging on the door, he realized immediately. His father had beaten them all out of bed and was already in the barn, giving the heifer some fresh hay. He stepped inside, pulled off his hat, and walked toward his father.

"Rawlings never came home last night," Mitchell said.

"You sure?"

"Yeah. Is anything wrong?"

"He had a date, and I wanted to talk something over with him—but I guess it can wait." He watched his father pat the cow on the forehead, then shoot him a curious glance.

"Anything I can help with?" Mitchell asked. Brandt gave him a tight smile. "I'm no Rawlings, but I can be a pretty good listener."

Brandt exhaled sharply and was just about to turn and run, tail tucked between his legs, when he thought better of it. "Look, Dad, I know you and I have never set aside much time to talk about personal stuff. We never had the 'birds and bees' talk."

Mitchell shook his head. "I didn't think it was necessary. I showed you how to turn a bull into a steer and that was that. You've seen a hundred calves being born, and even a few foals. In hindsight, though, I should've made the effort. You're my only son. You didn't seem to need as much, though. You were self-sufficient from an early age."

Brandt wanted to rebuke his father, tell him that he'd always needed more emotionally than Mitchell had been able or willing to provide. It would've been pretty stupid, though, and chicken-shit for a grown man to accuse his father of not being there for him. Even if Mitchell had kept him at arm's length, he was and had always been present. Things could've been a whole lot worse. "You know that Marissa and I have gotten close in a hurry."

Mitchell nodded. "That's been pretty easy to see."

"I love her, Dad." And despite his best efforts, Brandt frowned at the sentiment that escaped his lips. "And that scares me."

"Love is a pretty scary thing," Mitchell said. "But so is being alone."

"Remember how Marissa wanted to go to graduate school but she could never swing it, could never get accepted?" Mitchell nodded again. "Rowan has been encouraging her to apply to a different type of program, go more toward counseling instead of the therapy route. She could find a job in a school. But if she did go back to school, that would mean she would have to leave town."

"Are you mad?" Mitchell inquired, concern evident in his voice.

"Not at all," Brandt replied. "Well, maybe I'm mad at fate."

Mitchell laughed. "I think I understand that."

"I don't know if we could survive that, Dad. This is the girl that I want to marry." Mitchell's face perked up at the mention of marriage. "But we're talking two, maybe three years of barely seeing each other. How could a relationship survive that?" Brandt stamped around the barn, pacing in circles and curling the brim of his hat between his fingers. "I'm borrowing trouble from the future, huh? I'm worrying for nothing. This relationship just started."

"Settle down, son," Mitchell said, raising both hands in frustration. "You're gonna wear a hole in the floor." Which was impossible, since it was a dirt floor. "It's not like you don't have a driver's license and a truck. You'll just have to drive up there and see her wherever she is, when you can spare a weekend. You've also got the luxury of having a flexible schedule."

Brandt shot him a befuddled look. "Help me out here, Dad."

Mitchell took in a deep breath, his forehead wrinkling as he resumed his line of wisdom. "I need you here on the ranch, which is no secret. My hope is you'll wanna take charge of the place someday."

"I do," Brandt reassured him.

"It's not your typical nine-to-five job. More like six-to-six or thereabouts. My point, though, which is getting lost in the weeds, is that you only have to answer to me. If I wanna give you a whole week off, I'll do it. In the meantime, though, I need you to do something for me."

Brandt nodded, half out of breath from simultaneously listening to his father and letting his mind race. "What's that, Dad?"

"Show some commitment," he answered simply. "Prove to me that you're committed to Marissa. Bring her around the ranch when you can. Hell, take her out and show her how to sling bales of hay if you want to."

Brandt didn't tell his father that Marissa had pretty strong arms—an asset in bed, and on the ranch at some point in the future. Instead, he smiled and said, "I will, Dad. And thanks for the talk. I know it was a little dodgy in places, but I'm glad for your advice." He seated his hat atop his head. "Always."

Mitchell nodded and smiled before an unfamiliar emotion, one Brandt had rarely seen expressed, seemed to alter his face. "I'm here for you, son. Anytime you need me." Brandt nodded, met his father's eyes one last time, and headed outside. Rawlings was putting a key in the door of the bunkhouse, wearing last night's clothes, when he caught Brandt's gaze.

"Boy, do I have a story for you," he said.

Chapter Thirteen

Brandt's curiosity had been piqued with the news Rawlings never made it home the night before. Now it blossomed into full-blown nosiness as he followed his friend past the front door, closing it behind him. Both men rested their hats atop the kitchen counter as Rawlings hit the fridge and grabbed a bottle of water. He offered one to Brandt, but he declined with a wave of his hand.

"I spent the night with Rowan," Rawlings said once he'd downed half the bottle.

"No wonder you're so thirsty," Brandt said drolly.

"Ha-ha," Rawlings answered just as wryly. "Good one." But then he smiled, and looked like a man who'd just tossed the weight of the world off his shoulders. "We went to the same place you took for Marissa for your first date."

"Swear to God," Brandt said. "That catfish is an aphrodisiac."

"Maybe," Rawlings said with a laugh. "Anyway, we went back to her place afterward and she invited me inside."

"Did you…"

"Bring along protection? Yeah. I wanted it, but that doesn't mean I was expecting it." Brandt watched him smile and go inside his own head for a few minutes. "It was hot, and then we slowed down and it was kind of…"

"Sensual?" Brandt offered. "Intimate?"

"Yeah," he said again. "All of those fancy words."

"I'm going to ask Marissa to marry me."

Rawlings did a double take and met his friend with unguarded curiosity. "You serious?" Brandt nodded and recounted what'd happened two nights before, when he discovered the brochure in her apartment. He filled in everything that'd been discussed afterward, finally segueing into his conversation with his father a few minutes earlier. "I got a bad feeling about this, man. Not wanting to marry her, of course—you guys are clearly in love—but the long-distance mess. I don't envy you."

"I'm jumping the gun on this." Brandt planted himself in one of the mismatched chairs and let out a huge gust of air.

"Aw, hell, Brandt, you've always been quick on the draw. That's why people like you—you're a no nonsense, no bullshit kinda guy. If you think you're in love after less than a month, then I figure you probably are." Rawlings dispatched the empty bottle and took his standard place on the couch.

"This scares the hell out of me," Brandt admitted with a grimace.

"It should."

That caused Brandt to raise his brows. "Really?"

"Look," Rawlings said, twiddling his thumbs, "I don't know much about that whole love thing—there wasn't a whole lot of it when I was growing up, except what I saw around here."

Brandt laughed. "I hate to think we're your frame of reference."

Rawlings shrugged. "I don't. You're the best surrogate family I could've had."

His throat thick with emotion, Brandt simply nodded and elected to change the subject. "So when's the next date?"

He grinned. "Soon, man—real soon." He went silent as his mind conjured something. "You ever made it with just your hat on?"

Brandt feigned confusion, then cocked his head to one side and from the corner of his mouth said, "A few times." He braced his hands on the arms of the chair and stood. "You ready to head across the ranch?" he asked, pointing one thumb toward the door.

Rawlings nodded and was off the couch in a split-second. "Lead the way, pal."

•••

Marissa tapped her fingers against the table in a vain attempt to get Brandt's attention. He was clearly occupied, his mind as far away as the moon and the stars. They were on the opposite side of the restaurant from the sunlight, and his profile was thrown in shadows, the line of his chin clearly visible as he stared out the window.

"Brandt?"

"Hmm?" he answered, not bothering to meet her gaze.

"Cowboy?"

"Hmm?" Same response.

"Where the hell you at?" At last his head turned and their eyes met.

"Sorry," he said, his eyes conveying the genuine sentiment of contrition. "I was thinking about a bunch of different things. My head's pretty full right now."

"I understand," she said, nodding. "Rawlings and Rowan?"

He nodded. "And the ranch."

"And us?"

He nodded again. "And us."

She responded with a tight smile. "First things first," she said. "You okay with our best friends hooking up?"

He shrugged, gave her his best noncommittal smile. "As long as they're happy, I'm happy. He got to spend the whole night with her, which means he's already one-up on me."

"Don't sell yourself short, Brandt." His smile was a little more playful now. "We manage to pack a lot of fun into just a few hours."

"We do that, don't we?" His left eyebrow lifted almost imperceptibly, the look of a rascal—her rascal.

"What about the ranch?" she urged. "Problems?"

Brandt shook his head. "Not really. I just want us to be practical about it. This is my life, and I'm committed to it. I won't forget to love you, but some days are so tough that you forget to show someone what they mean to you."

"I'm used to playing second fiddle to a cow," she joked. "I work for Mona, remember?"

They laughed together, and her face burned when he gave her a huge smile. "I don't think it's normal to love so deep, so fast, Marissa."

She reached across the table until her hand was resting in his. "When is love ever normal?" she questioned him. "Think about the number of people who get divorced every year. A lot of them probably went into it thinking life was going to be normal and happy. Then it wasn't."

"No one has all the answers," Brandt murmured.

"Exactly." He smiled at her, but she saw the anxiety carefully formed at the corners of his mouth. Earlier in the meal she'd discussed both her application and admissions essay. She'd submit it on Monday, and wait for confirmation from the various people from whom she'd solicited letters of recommendation. It had been a very good idea, she thought, to maintain close contacts with those professors with whom she'd worked side-by-side.

"I never would've been able to do all of that," Brandt had told her. "I did the course work to the best of my ability, but I didn't spend much time getting to know the teachers." As well as Brandt knew her, she kept a few things hidden from him—that she was a natural introvert, a hard worker who'd been born shy and stayed that way for most of her life. Making contacts while in college was one thing, but Brandt was one of the few people to whom she'd ever opened up on a personal level. She knew he possessed opinions, but regarding her he'd been pretty damned non-judgmental. And that, she realized, was a Godsend.

"So what about us?" she asked yet again.

He squeezed her hand between his thumb and palm. "Whatever comes our way, whether or not grad school happens for you, we're in it for the long haul. I'm not letting you get away."

"I wish I had your confidence," she said with a frown. "This whole thing feels kind of surreal."

"It's scary. Believe me, Marissa—I understand that. I get how you're feeling."

"Because you're feeling the same way?"

His tough-as-nails exterior cracked just a bit, and she saw the tender side that he usually reserved for their private moments. "Yeah," he said hoarsely. "I love you, Marissa. I'm already sure that I want to spend the rest of my life with you. But I also know that loving someone means you want what's best for them." His voice came out clear as a bell, cutting through the din of the restaurant. "I'd like to think I'm someone you can count on."

"You are," she stated emphatically, and he smiled. "I'm very lucky to have found you."

Brandt laughed. "I'm the one who found you, remember? I was shopping that day."

She nodded, a smirk coming to her lips. "Yes," she recalled. "That was one time that I didn't mind being checked out."

• • •

"I'm sure this isn't what you had in mind," Marissa said.

Brandt laughed, wrapped his arm around her shoulders, and pulled her closer to him atop the blanket. He'd backed his truck onto the creek bank, the bed hanging over the water, and they'd climbed into the back to watch the stars fill the sky. So while it hadn't been his first choice, it had been his idea. "What do you mean?" he asked with mock affront. "This is a perfect way to spend an evening."

"It is nice," she said. Her snuggling into his shoulder felt nice too. He put his lips to her eyebrow and placed a kiss above her left eye.

"If you could wish on a star and have it come true," he asked, "what would you wish for?"

"A pair of alligator boots," she joked.

He ran one hand down her elbow and laughed. He glanced into her eyes, their color imperceptible in the darkness. "Be serious."

"Oh, I don't know," she said with some hesitance. "I'd like to know my dad aside from just a piece of paper, the man who sends birthday cards. But his absence shaped me into the person I am today. I might never have been so strong-willed were I not raised by such a capable mother, who was strong because she had to be. You've helped too."

He brushed his lips over hers. "Is that right?"

"Yes. I love you, Brandt, so much that I can feel it deep inside. Does that make any sense?"

He nodded, because he understood completely. He loved Marissa to the point that she'd seeped into his marrow. It was little wonder that sex between them was so incredible—she was the missing piece of the puzzle, the answer to a question he'd forgotten to ask. "Yeah, sweetheart," he answered hoarsely. "It makes perfect sense."

She pulled herself further into his chest, resting atop him now. She kissed him ardently, then deepened it, her mouth sweet and pliant as it melded with his. It was almost enough to make him forgot about the chill in the air. "We're not going to make love in the bed of your truck, are we?" she murmured against his lips. He fought to stifle a laugh.

"Not tonight," he replied, "but when it gets warmer, hell yes."

"I'll look forward to that," she assured him. They separated, their eyes drifting heavenward again. "Brandt?" she asked a minute later.

"I'm listening, beautiful."

"What do you wish for, when you look at the stars?"

He thought on it, but only for a few seconds. His answer came readily to mind. "I wish that my parents would be around long enough to spoil their grandkids. I wish that Rawlings could find the happiness he's always deserved. And I wish all your dreams could come true."

"Nothing for yourself?"

He laughed softly. "I wish for a thousand more nights just like this one."

• • •

"Now that I have you right where I want you…"

Brandt laughed. "I know where this is headed."

With her hips straddling him, Marissa kissed her way up his chest, her hands and lips gliding their way across the expanse of skin and muscle. His body was still flushed red, and goose flesh broke out when she kissed the hardened flesh of his upper arm. As great as it was to make love, to move with him as Brandt labored atop her, the after part was always pretty great too. He'd kiss away the beads of sweat that invariably formed on her stomach, or she'd massage his shoulders, his back, or some point lower—he never complained, no matter what she chose to do. When his face wore the mask of contentment, of unending love and easy tenderness, was when he was the most handsome. She rested her forearm across his chest and swallowed.

"What's that all about?" he asked, lifting his chin as one hand brushed strands of hair away from her cheek. "You gave me that look."

"What look might that be?" she asked, narrowing her eyes.

He grinned in response to her evasion. "You get this startled look, like you can't believe I'm real."

She was disquieted by his accurate read of the situation. "Sometimes I forget how beautiful you are," she said.

He lifted his head up and kissed her until they were out of breath. "That's my line, remember? I'm pretty sure that God never made a more beautiful woman than you."

"You could sell matches to people in Hell, you know that?" He grinned up at her, a stray lock of hair attacking his forehead. She laughed and brushed it back into place. "Anyway, have you ever been curious about where I get my looks?"

Brandt's face scrunched up in confusion. "You weren't born with them?" Truth be told, there wasn't much spare fat on his body, but her fingers pinched a small segment of his arm—the same place where her lips had just been—and he laughed in surprise.

"Don't forget that I can do serious damage to you, Brandt Conner," she said in a teasing manner. Marissa blinked her eyelids rapidly. "I want you to meet my mother."

"When?" he asked.

"That's it?" she replied. "No drama, no debates, no fighting?"

She could feel his chest vibrate from laughter. "First of all, I love you. Second, I happen to love the position your body is in relative to mine." An obvious twinkle lit up his eyes. "And third, I'd be honored to meet the woman who raised such a fine daughter."

"She's got plenty of built-up vacation days, and I've just about convinced her to take a Friday off and come up here to visit me. Hopefully she'd stay the weekend."

He nodded, and she felt his hands slide onto her, bracketing her hips. "I like the sound of that." He pulled her closer. "And I like the feel of this."

She brushed her lips across his chin. "Never let it be said that you don't have a one-track mind, Brandt Conner."

He rolled atop her, pausing for a moment of reflection. "If I had a one-track mind, Miss Sloan, we'd be doing none of this talking." His eyes burned brighter now.

"Then why are we still talking?" she asked, one eyebrow lifted skeptically.

"Honestly?" he answered. "Your voice turns me on." And with the welcome pressure of his lips, he brought their conversation to a swift end.

Chapter Fourteen

Brandt loaded his shell, snapped the gun together, and sighted the paper target. It was attached to a foam backing which would capture the ammunition once he'd made his shot. One thing Mitchell had taught his son—never fire at random. No target, no shooting. Rawlings stood a safe distance away, putting in his earplugs now that Brandt stood at the ready. He looked down the barrel, and fired until he was out of shots. He snapped open the break action and let the empty shells fall to the ground.

"I hope you ain't that quick in bed," Rawlings joked.

Brandt grinned at him. "I'll try to keep from bragging about my pump action and the number of shells I've always got in reserve. After all, Marissa is coming over today."

Rawlings nodded. "I can tell. Your smile is even bigger than usual."

Brandt laughed. "You gonna come in the house and have lunch with us?"

"Sure am. Marissa thinks I'm part of the family too."

"You are part of the family," Brandt reminded him. Rawlings smiled a little sheepishly at him, clearly humbled, and Brandt decided to shift gears. "What'd you do last night? You and Rowan go out on a date?"

"Nope," he said, a grin forming on his lips. "I took a bag of groceries over to her apartment and made dinner."

"That was nice of you."

"Uh-huh, and it's your fault, Conner."

He laughed, not needing the reason but asking it anyway. "And why is that?"

"Because you told her about my cooking skills on the first date!" he answered rapidly, his voice shooting up a few octaves.

"Oh yeah," Brandt deadpanned. "I remember that now." He tapped his thumb against the wooden stock of his gun. "So, really, you should be thanking me, McCoy, for getting you laid."

Rawlings glared at him, open-mouthed, but then switched back to a smile. "Thank you for being my wingman. But it was my natural charm and rugged good looks that got my foot in the door."

Brandt nodded. "I'll agree to that." The conversation trailed off then, both men casting their gazes down to the dirt. "So..."

Rawlings lifted his chin. "You nervous about meeting Marissa's mom?"

"I'd be lying if I said I wasn't. She has to be a pretty amazing woman, bringing up Marissa single-handedly like she did."

"You never know what you're capable of until you have to do it," Rawlings surmised. "I think I could've left home either way, but having a place to come to really helped." He smiled crookedly. "A place to land."

"I guess we need to bring Rowan out here, show her around the place," Brandt suggested. "Let her see what we do for a living when we're not swaggering into town."

Rawlings laughed. "Not a bad idea, man—although with school letting out soon, she'd have time to be around every day."

• • •

Marissa was putting her vacation days to good use. She was still secretly relieved that Mona had granted them in the first place, although the mention of Connie's name had helped matters. Marissa was still curious about the nature of their friendship, which made little sense to her. Maybe she'd have the opportunity to ask about it tomorrow.

Today, though, she was heading out to the ranch to spend some time with Brandt. That wasn't her only purpose, though—she planned to spend a few minutes with Brandt's mother. Laura reminded Marissa in many ways of her own mother—two women who made the best of what they had and always managed a smile.

Marissa felt at peace as she drove onto the ranch and parked near the house. The place was fully alive now with emerald-colored grass and leaves that shook with the wind and gave the place an air of fortification. It was as though the lush foliage protected them from the outside world—and it made the cows pretty damned happy too. She stepped out of the car and heard the clucking of hens beneath their coop. She tried not to let it startle her when she then heard gunshots coming from behind the house—Brandt had warned her beforehand that he and Rawlings would be out there, doing a little reconnaissance prior to hunting season. She'd been amused by his choice of words.

She knocked on the door, which Laura promptly answered. She was smiling as he ushered Marissa in, wiping her hands on her apron. "It's just us girls today, Marissa," she said as they walked through the house, the floors creaking with each step. "I assume you heard the boys out back?"

"I did."

"And Mitchell is in town doing…something or other."

Marissa laughed as they entered the kitchen. "Something to do with the ranch?" she assumed.

"Yes, that sounds right." Laura smiled and pulled out a spare apron. Marissa went to wash her hands at the sink. "I guess you should be aware of what your husband is doing, and I know he told me, but we've been married for so many years that our habits are by rote. If he's going into town, I know it's something important."

"If you don't mind my asking, Mrs. Conner…"

"Laura, please," she insisted.

"How long have you and Mr. Conner been married?" She tied the strings together and waited for Laura to answer. She seemed flustered, perhaps at the question, or the matter of time. Maybe, Marissa thought, she'd simply forgotten.

"Thirty-two years," she finally said. "We were married at eighteen, and it was several more years before Brandt came along. It seems like a lifetime ago, but I also have a hard time remembering my life before I was a mother. Maybe that's the way it should be." She pulled a cookbook from one of the cabinets, its cover and pages timeworn, dog-eared, and stained from food spills. "Brandt tells me your mother is coming for a visit tomorrow."

Marissa nodded. "That's right. Truthfully, I'm kind of excited. I haven't seen her for a month, but it feels like much longer."

Laura looked up from the cookbook long enough to smile warmly at her. "The bond between mother and child is like nothing else in the world, but the bond between a mother and an only child is a particularly special one. I know something about that."

"Brandt told me that you and Mitchell actually wanted more children. I hope that's okay for him to share that piece of information."

"It's fine," Laura assured her. "Because it's true. Mitchell and I would have liked a houseful of children. Instead, God saw fit to only bless me with one pregnancy, and I never questioned Him. It makes you fearful, though. Luckily Brandt and I have always had a close relationship. It's even more remarkable when you consider the amount of time he spent outside of this house and with his father."

"I may be overstepping my bounds here, but the relationship between Brandt and Mitchell—it's strained?"

"It's complex," Laura confirmed. "Can I share something with you in confidence?" Marissa nodded. "As they get older, both of them are becoming more set in their ways, and that scares me. It's like one of those nature shows on television where you see two rams slamming into each other, butting horns. They fight until their horns break, or one of them is exhausted."

"Sometimes their horns lock together and they die like that," Marissa recalled with a frown.

"Yes," Laura said, nodding sadly. "Okay. Let's move onto something a little happier. How are you in the kitchen?"

"I'm fair," Marissa admitted. "No offense, but I think I'm better than Brandt."

Laura simply laughed. "Good—that means you'll never starve. If you're willing, I'd like to share some recipes with you. As far as cooking goes, Brandt is definitely a carnivore."

Marissa smiled. "Good to know."

"Many of these recipes I know by heart," Laura informed her. "Don't tell my husband, though—he thinks I invented blackberry cobbler."

"It'll be our secret."

She watched as Laura made biscuits from scratch—a process Marissa had never seen before. Flour was sifted out carefully, but somehow managed to dust their faces and the countertop. Every now and then both women would jump at the sound of shells being spent. "I really should be used to that by now," Laura said. A few minutes later she mixed together a colander full of blackberries she told Marissa she had frozen the previous summer with enough sugar to form syrup. "The berries grow wild here on our property, but only the part where the cattle don't roam. Cows have a habit of eating anything green or floral, you know."

Marissa placed the biscuits evenly atop the fruit mixture, then slid the glass pan into the oven. She went to push the hair away from her face before remembering it had been in a ponytail all morning.

"Go outside and see Brandt now if you'd like, dear. I can take care of things in here."

"Thank you, Laura," she said, smiling as she untied her apron and left it atop the counter. She hoped it didn't seem rude that she practically bolted through the kitchen and out the back door—then again, Laura had been the one to suggest it.

Brandt turned and looked at her—he cut a dashing figure, she thought, the gun broken in half and slung over his shoulder like he was some kind of movie cowboy ready for a high-noon showdown. He gave her a huge smile, and Rawlings touched the brim of his hat as a show of respect. "You great white hunters heading into the woods, or just practicing?"

"A little of both," Brandt replied, still smiling.

"We're gonna try to bag a turkey this year," Rawlings added. "Easier said than done."

"I didn't interrupt, did I?"

"No, ma'am," Rawlings assured her. "I was just getting ready to check on the cattle. Later, you two."

"Take it easy, partner," Brandt said. When Rawlings's back was to them, Brandt pulled Marissa into a kiss. "I was starting to get worried about you. Mom didn't bore you with old baby pictures, did she?"

Marissa pressed her thumb into his chin. "I've already seen those photos, and you were adorable in them."

"I'm better looking now," he joked.

"That goes without saying," she assured him. "No, we were cooking. Your name may have entered the conversation once or twice."

"I think Mom fell in love with you just as quickly as I did." He dropped his chin and kissed her on the forehead. "Then again, how could anyone not fall in love with you? You're so damned perfect."

"Perfect for you," she reminded him.

"Damned straight," he drawled, cutting off her words with his lips. He was good at that, she thought cheerfully—very, very good. He pulled away long enough to kneel to the ground, scoop up the empty shells, and toss them in a bucket. "So, tomorrow," he said.

"Tomorrow," she confirmed. His smile warmed her all the way through—his support meant more to her than she could put into words.

He nodded and held her hand as they headed for the house. "I'll be there."

• • •

Around mid-morning, Brandt parked his truck outside of Marissa's apartment and took the stairs two at a time. There was a strange car parked outside, and thanks to the Tennessee plates he pegged it immediately as her mother's car. He knocked at the door and Marissa smiled as she led him toward the living room. "This is my mother," she said. "Mom, this is Brandt."

Connie Sloan was a slight woman, shorter than her daughter, with similar features set in a timeworn face—the same blue in her eyes, and a lighter blonde hue on her short hair, clearly touched-up but, Brandt figured, professionally done. He took her small, work-roughened hand in his and shook it. "Pleased to make your acquaintance, ma'am."

She smiled, seemingly pleased at his formality. "It's nice to finally meet you, Brandt."

"Why don't we take a seat?" Marissa offered. Brandt sat down facing them, adjusting his legs nervously. Marissa shot him a bemused grin. "We just finished up some leftover cobbler."

"I'd love if your mother would share the recipe with me," Connie said.

139

Brandt chuckled. "She'd be more than willing, but she'd also be the first to tell you that it came straight out of a cookbook."

"The blackberries were the easy part," Marissa recalled. "It was the topping that required a steady hand."

Uneasy silence settled onto the room after that comment. "So, Brandt," Connie began, "Marissa tells me that you're a rancher."

"I can't brag," Brandt told her. "My dad is the real rancher. I just help out."

"Don't let him fool you, Mom," Marissa said. "He does a pretty fair share of the work. He's a born cattleman."

"My best friend is the de facto ranch foreman," Brandt countered, "so it's a three-man operation."

"Do you make a good living at it?" Connie asked, then placed a hand to her mouth in humiliation. "I'm sorry if I spoke out of turn."

Brandt smiled easily. "You didn't, Ms. Sloan. Yes, we do pretty well for ourselves, but most of it goes back into the ranch. The house is old, and none of our vehicles are new. We buy hay and feed, but we grow most of our own vegetables. One thing's for sure—with a bunch of cattle and a few chickens running around, you're never gonna starve."

Connie nodded, clearly satisfied with that answer. "Marissa also tells me that you are highly supportive of her educational goals."

"Absolutely," he said with a brief nod. "Her happiness is my main concern."

"Which is a rare quality, Brandt, I have to tell you. In marriage, it seems that one spouse always winds up compromising more than the other one."

"I know it won't be easy to keep this thing together when Marissa goes off to school, but it will be worth it."

"When?" she repeated.

Marissa jumped into the conversation, her eyes still locked on him as she spoke. "Brandt is very confident in my ability to be accepted. In fact, you might say he's my biggest advocate."

"Have you two thought seriously about marriage?" Connie wondered aloud.

"I have," Brandt answered. Marissa's eyebrow shot upward. "I'm sure this all seems very soon, but when it's right, you know it. We're both adults, and our feelings for one another are pretty strong."

"I'm not trying to talk you out of anything," Connie said reassuringly. "I just want you to think about how difficult it is to maintain a relationship over the long-haul."

"I know it will be difficult," Brandt reiterated, "but nothing worth having ever comes easy."

"No, you're right," Connie agreed with a small smile. "And you should also know that I didn't come all the way up here to give you the third degree. I would, however, like you to join us for lunch today."

Brandt let his lungs empty of the air he'd been hoarding, and then he laughed. "I'd like that too, but only if you'll let me pay."

"Nonsense!" came her quick reply. "If you're planning to get married, you'll have to get used to never winning an argument again." She excused herself, and Marissa came toward Brandt and knelt down to give him a kiss.

"And now you know where I get my charming personality," she said, resting on the chair arm.

He wet her lips, then laughed again. "That became clear about five seconds after I met her," he joked, and she tugged playfully on his cheek in reply.

Chapter Fifteen

Brandt spent much of Friday with Marissa and her mother, though he left prior to dinner. On Saturday morning they went shopping at the flea market, amongst other places, and Connie enjoyed catching up with Rowan. Marissa was glad to see her mother in such good spirits, and was glad that she genuinely liked Brandt. Parental approval may not have been necessary for a relationship, but it certainly didn't hurt. By Saturday evening they were dining at an Italian restaurant, and as Marissa drizzled house dressing over her salad, she finally worked up the courage to ask the question that had been burning in her mind for a while now.

"Mom?"

Connie looked at her expectantly. "What is it, sweetie?"

"How did you become friends with Mona Larkin?"

Connie's face changed, shifting from hopeful to somewhat surprised. "You remember that she and I attended school together?" Marissa nodded. Connie folded her napkin across her lap and sighed. "We were assigned a project in which we had to read a novel and complete a report and a diorama. I'm glad dioramas have become a thing of the past for schoolchildren. They were truly horrible. Anyway, Mona's parents were having serious marital problems and she was deeply affected by their strife. Her grades suffered in every class, but English was the worst. She was near to failing, and told me that the teacher said the report and diorama were a make-or-break situation. If she failed to complete them—if *we* failed to complete them—she likely would have been held back an entire year."

"So what happened?" Marissa inquired. "You wound up doing all the work?"

"Not exactly," her mother clarified. The main course arrived and they paused the conversation long enough to thank the waiter and compliment the food's appearance. Twirling pasta around her fork, she resumed the story. "Mona's family had more money than mine did, so she bought all of the supplies and I completed the diorama. And, honey, I am grateful for that, because I got an A-plus on it."

"What about the report?"

"Of the two of us, her writing was marginally better. I completed the book, along the way crafting a study guide, and she wrote the report. We were later quizzed over the finer points of the book, and both of us passed. Mona passed the course, and I, for once, handed in a project that didn't look to have been fashioned from scotch tape and spit."

"She really owed you big after that," Marissa said, taken aback by not only her mother's candor but also Mona's unhappy past. Could that have been the reason for her continued unpleasantness, despite a solid marriage and family of her own?

Connie shrugged. "Well, maybe. I only called in my favor because of you. I didn't have a leg to stand on, honestly—it was hardly blackmail—but I think she also remembered that I was kind to her during a time in her life where she had nowhere to turn. And so you have to remember, if she seems brittle, it's because her life was shattered. Her parents reconciled, but some marriages are like a broken piece of glass—you can glue it back together, but the fissure will always be there."

Marissa nodded. "What happened with you and Dad? Why did he leave and never come back?"

Connie had begun to eat, but now she laid down her fork and sighed. "It's like I've told you before—we were just too young, and inexperienced, and the realities of marriage didn't line up with his notions or ideas of what it should be." She narrowed her eyes. "Some men should never marry, sweetheart, and that's the truth. Max Sloan is one of those men. I think he allowed his libido to get in the way of his ambition, and came to regret it once the ring was on my finger and you were born."

"I wish I could better understand him," Marissa said, shaking her head. She ate for a minute, chewing on food, chewing on her thoughts about the man who'd sired and then abandoned her. "The birthday cards and the money he sends—guilt, or did he have a genuine attachment to me?"

Connie smiled. "This is going to sound like a copout, but I think your father loves you, or maybe just the idea of you. He told me that if he stayed, he would have ruined all of our lives, and that we were better off without him."

"That's definitely a copout on his part," Marissa said decisively. "He forced us to become a single-income family, and ensured that you would always be stuck in that factory."

"I'm not apologizing for his actions, but I like to think I did a pretty good job of raising you on my own."

Marissa thought about what she knew of Rawlings and his unhappy upbringing—having two parents around, and a bunch of siblings, was no guarantee of either stability or nurturing. "You did, Mom. You absolutely did."

• • •

Brandt was in the living room, a book open in his lap, when his mother came in from church. In truth, he only gave the outward appearance of reading the novel—he'd read the same paragraph three times now without comprehending it or advancing to another page. He might just as well stretch out on the couch, rest his hat atop his face, and go to sleep.

Laura removed her wrap and laid it across the couch arm—Brandt figured they'd turned on the A/C at church prematurely—and took a seat near him. "Where's Dad?" he asked.

"Out in the barn, checking on his calf," she said with a smile.

"Did you enjoy meeting Marissa's mom?" Mitchell and Laura had been scheduled to have lunch with Marissa and Connie following church and before she returned home.

Laura nodded. "I did. She is a very lovely woman and had plenty of nice things to say about you."

His eyebrows perked up. "About me?"

"Yes, you, humble boy." She laughed. "She made it clear that she not only is in awe of how much you love her daughter, but also that she considers you a good influence on Marissa."

Brandt closed the book, laid it atop the end table, and shook his head. "Marissa doesn't need my guiding hand, Mom. Everything she wants, everything she dreams about and can achieve, is already inside her. Maybe I'm just good at drawing it out."

"You're not a child anymore, and you don't need me to tell you this, but having someone love you is a big help in life."

He smiled at her wisdom, knowing her words were correct. "Did I tell you that she was admitted? Not to the graduate program yet, but the university itself. That means she can start taking courses as soon as tomorrow."

"That was fast," Laura noted. "But I'm glad."

"Me too," he said halfheartedly. His mother shot him a knowing gaze. "What?" he asked softly.

She had already slipped out of her heels and was now reaching down to massage her feet. "Marissa might be moving away for college, and Rawlings is spending most of his free time with Rowan. You can't convince me that neither of those things bothers you." When he opened his mouth in a denial that got lodged somewhere in his throat, she continued. "I nursed you through colic, teething, night terrors, and a broken leg."

That got Brandt's attention. "I had night terrors?"

Laura nodded. "Until you were six years old. I'd wake up and run to your room just as you started screaming."

"And I stopped?"

She nodded again. "I guess you grew out of them. From then on, you tried to maintain the appearance of a man who was in control of his fears."

"At the age of six?" he asked incredulously.

"Yes," she said with a laugh. "At the age of six." She smiled at him with great affection. "But I always knew the difference. When they put your leg in that cast, and when you went off to college the first time, there was something behind your eyes. I hid my own anxiety because it wouldn't have done any good to share it. And you're fully grown now, but you still live under my roof. I'm rambling, but the point I'm trying to make is that you have to prepare yourself for the changes life will bring."

Brandt looked downward, away from his mother, losing himself in a moment of contemplation. His fear of loneliness—paranoia, really—was getting the better of him. "Mom?"

"Yes, sweetheart?" she answered immediately.

"You really are the best, you know that?"

She smiled, and he noted the emotion clouding her eyes. "I had a good son—that helps. Brandt?" she added, almost as an afterthought.

"Yeah?"

"You don't have to sacrifice your own happiness to guarantee someone else's. You can have both—it just may arrive in a different form than you'd expected." With that, she grabbed her shoes and headed out of the room. "I'm going to start on dinner," she said matter-of-factly. "Do you need anything?"

"No," he replied languidly. "I'm going to go check on Dad."

Laura nodded. "I think that's a fine idea."

Brandt smiled. "Thanks, Mom."

And even though he hadn't been specific about his gratitude, she smiled in return and said, "You're welcome."

Brandt stood, let out a deep breath, and adjusted his hat. On the way out to the barn, he texted Marissa. So much for his plan to give her ample space this weekend.

•••

Marissa tried to maintain the façade, but with each passing second it became more difficult. She and Connie were standing between the two cars, the parking lot suddenly feeling forlorn and desolate. It was sunny, the birds singing, the air clean and fresh. Only the occasional car noise from the road cut through an otherwise-bucolic atmosphere.

"Is it strange that I don't want this weekend to come to an end?" she asked unevenly. "I miss you already."

Connie gave her an understanding look, then pulled her daughter into her arms and brushed her hands across Marissa's hair, in the same calming way she'd done when she was a child and life's problems seemed so much harder to take. "I already miss you too, but I know that I don't have to worry as much. You've surrounded yourself with good people, and you have a man in your life that loves you—*loves you*," she emphasized. "Brandt is very special."

"I know, Mom," she said, her throat thickening as the words came out. "I just wish you lived closer and we could be together more often."

Connie tapped her on the end of the nose. "You know, you could call a bit more often. I'm just a few keystrokes away." Marissa laughed.

"That is true, but I think you deserve to rest when you come home from work. My days are so…mundane."

"What about when you're with Brandt?" she mused.

"Need-to-know," Marissa replied, and they both laughed. "Okay, I want you home before dark."

"Don't try to tell me what to do, young lady," Connie joked, but her hand was already on the door. "I'll call you as soon as I get there," she promised.

"Good," Marissa said. "I love you, Mom."

"I love you too, sweetie." They hugged and kissed and Marissa waved until her mother drove out of sight. She stood there and sighed. Then she cried a few tears, but vowed they would be gone by the time Brandt arrived.

She was seated outside her door, reading a course syllabus she'd printed and stuck to a clipboard, when he pulled up and parked at the bottom of the steps. He opened his door, glanced upward, and smiled when he immediately found her. Relief washed through her veins at the sight of him—never in her life had she been able to count on a man. Somehow Brandt had changed all of that.

When he got to the top of the stairs, she stood, and he pulled her into a firm hug. His touch was gentle and powerful, his index finger lifting her chin upward. "Your eyes are a little red, but you don't look any worse for the wear," he observed.

"Mom wouldn't let me cry until she left," Marissa replied. Brandt laughed so hard that the sound filled her insides too.

"I hear that our parents got along very well," he mentioned.

"Yes, that's true," she said, staring up into his eyes. The shadows had turned their irises into a darker hue of green, the color rich and mysterious. "I mean, you inherited your charm from somewhere."

He laughed again, gave her a crooked smile. "And here I thought it came from eating too many carrots."

"Well, maybe," she teased, and her face flushed when he responded with a huge grin.

"You know what this means, don't ya?"

"Hmm," she said. "Give me a hint."

Brandt cleared his throat, and his face and voice took on an authoritative tone. Truth be told, she loved when he seemingly "lectured" her. "When the parents get along, you're totally free to get married. That's, like, the last hurdle."

She rested one hand atop his chest, felt his heart pounding through his ribs. "Two hurdles remain, Brandt."

"Only two?" he asked hopefully.

She pretended to glare at him. "One, we've been dating for all of a month."

"Yeah, but we've had a lot of great sex during that time."

She smiled in spite of herself, wondering how anyone could speak of sex with such a childlike, impish grin on their face. "Point taken."

"What the second thing?" he asked, his countenance changing yet again to one that was more adult and mature.

"You haven't asked me yet," she reminded him.

"Oh," he said, teasing her as he drawled out the word. "Well, I asked for your hand already."

"When?" she said, her mouth agape. She imagined she resembled a largemouth bass at that moment—hook not included.

"You excused yourself to go to the restroom. I turned to Connie and said, 'How about it?' and she answered, 'Thank you for taking her off my hands, it's been a long wait.'" He burst out laughing and she slapped him playfully on the chest. He grabbed her by the shoulders and dragged her mouth to his again and again, cutting off protests she was unwilling to give. Each kiss was hot and sweet, and better than the one that came before. When she felt like her lungs would explode from lack of air, he pulled away and gave her a long, lingering once-over. "I really did ask for your hand, and she was fine with it. I've still gotta buy the ring and make up my mind about it."

"How about I help you along?" she offered.

"Oh?" he said, his eyes sweeping toward the door now.

"Yes," she said, taking him by the hand. "I've just about perfected my powers of persuasion."

Chapter Sixteen

If Brandt had spent more time in Sunday school, or under the church roof, he might have remembered something about the sin of pride. He also might have remembered that life can change in an instant, and understood that when things seemed too perfect, it couldn't last. As the weeks passed, though, everything hummed along nicely. Marissa's free time was more limited, but he still looked forward to just being in her presence. He'd sit on her couch, his ankle crossed over his knee, and watch her at the computer, reading notes and submitting assignments. She'd chewed on a pen when she thought no one was looking, her brow furrowed adorably as she concentrated on the task at hand. She was the damnedest woman he'd ever laid eyes on—she could manage to look sexy in bed, or with a simple smile, or when she was frustrated as hell.

Little wonder he was considering marriage. Marissa was the complete package.

"Brandt Conner," she said, startling him out of his thoughts. "Are you staring at me again?"

He smiled apologetically. "Guilty as charged, ma'am." Their eyes met, and he lifted one brow at her. "I could leave if it bothers you?" He pretended to stand, and she raised a hand to stop him.

"No," she said, smiling that gentle, pensive smile that drove him crazy. "I like having you here."

"And I like being here." She smiled again at his words, and returned her focus to the computer. "You'd better get used to it," he declared.

"And why is that?" she asked without turning around.

He shrugged, knowing she couldn't see him. "I guess I just like to look at you."

"That's sweet," she said appreciatively, before she drifted away from him yet again. He smiled.

He was, he knew, truly glad for Marissa. She was excelling in her first course, one of those accelerated four-week deals that required participation five days a week. How in the heck was she doing it all? She was working full-time, putting her full energy into this class, and dating him. It boggled his mind—in a good way. Just as his mother had predicted, life was quickly changing. With school out for the summer, Rowan was spending a lot of time with Rawlings, and her car was usually parked outside the bunkhouse when he woke up in the morning. If Mitchell or Laura minded an extra person on the ranch, neither of them said a word. Brandt figured they were as glad for his happiness as they were for their own son's. Everyone kept busy with the ranch too, and Brandt found himself extra-protective toward his mother's tomato plants. After all, those things had saved his life.

Marissa turned off her computer, obviously finished for now, and laid her chewed-up pen aside. She swiveled in the desk chair until she was facing him. "What's on your mind, Brandt? And don't try to tell me 'nothing.' I know you too well."

He smiled and nodded at her. Her words rang true—she knew him inside and out, his deepest fears and most of his flaws—and yet she loved him anyway. "I'm just kind of worried," he admitted. "About us."

She moved quickly, resting herself in his lap. He loved the feel of her in his arms, curled up like she'd been made to fit there. "Your fears are unfounded, cowboy."

"But I still have them," he answered hoarsely.

Her thumb brushed across his lips, igniting the fire deep inside him. "I'm scared about going to college," she said. "Again."

He struggled to clear his throat, overcome as he was by a litany of irrational fears. "You want to know something?"

"About you? Always."

"When I first went off to college, I was homesick as hell. For about a week I thought I'd made the biggest mistake of my life."

She met his gaze with curious eyes. "What finally changed your mind?"

"Nothing," he answered, shaking his head. "It just went away after a while. Maybe I have too much time to think," he wondered aloud.

"I guess that's my fault," she apologized.

"No, it's not," he countered. "I'm happy for Rawlings—God knows he deserves someone like Rowan in his life. It's just really different, not having him around to talk to at the end of a long day."

"You've still got me," she reminded him. He tightened his grip on her, and Marissa's head rested atop his left shoulder.

"I'm a lucky man," he said, his thumb massaging her neck. "Make sure I don't forget that."

•••

"What's taking so long?" Rowan teased. Marissa heard her boot heels clicking against the floor as she stuck her head in the bathroom.

"I'm still trying to figure out the right earrings to wear," she declared. She'd tried at least three pairs, but none seemed to coordinate with her turquoise blouse and faded jeans.

Rowan came up behind her, her fingers fumbling at her own ears. "Wear mine," she said. Marissa looked at them in surprise— they were long, with turquoise and brick red beads accented by silver.

"What about you?" she worried, slipping them into her ears.

"Give me the red ones you just had." Marissa handed them over and Rowan put them on. "Perfect—they go with my shirt."

The boys—or, more accurately, their men—were taking them dancing tonight. Marissa had decided that she and Rowan should work on each other's hair beforehand, and thus Brandt was swinging by to pick them up at Marissa's apartment. Both women were still in the bathroom when there was a loud knock at the door.

"Let's not keep them in suspense," Marissa said. When she pulled open the door to two men in pressed shirts and polished boots, she smiled as their faces changed expressions.

"Damn," Brandt said, "you are lookin' good tonight." He pulled her into his arms and lowered his mouth to her ear. "How about we dump the kids and have a night in, just you and me?" he whispered in a ragged voice.

"Take it easy," she said, running one hand along a cheek, feeling it bunch up in a smile. "Our friends are looking forward to a night on the town."

"Even if it is a trip to a cowboy bar," Rowan teased. Rawlings placed a wet kiss on her cheek and she laughed, clearly smitten with him.

"We are cowboys," he argued.

She winked and tugged on the brim of his hat. "How could I forget?"

They headed for the truck, the couples hand-in-hand, and piled in for the short drive to the other end of town. There were no smoky bars anymore—those days were gone due to health concerns and changing public opinion—but the place had maintained much of its old ambience. It had a ramshackle appearance, but Brandt assured the women it was safe—mostly.

"Think twice before using the restrooms," he said, pulling to a stop and shutting off the engine. Loud music immediately took over the air.

"Why's that?" Marissa asked, one eyebrow arched at him.

"Just trust us on this one," Rawlings said, leaning forward from the rear seat.

They made their way inside, and Marissa was pleasantly surprised. A few of the men there could have been brawlers, but the place was mostly filled with couples or friends hanging out after a long day's work. The music was predictably loud, and when Brandt asked her to join him on the dance floor, she had to strain to hear him—but his hand against the small of her back told her all she needed to know.

"I really needed this," she half-yelled at him. Their bodies were locked pretty tight together, and she heard a small laugh escape his throat.

"Then I'm glad I brought you," he said.

"School has really been kicking my ass lately," she said, which was partially true. Her midterm was coming up and she'd been studying like crazy, but her participation and assignment grades had all been perfect so far.

"You're doing great," Brandt countered, his hands sliding lower on her hips. "You're the smartest person I know."

"Because I'm dating you?"

"Well," he said, grinning, "that's one reason."

"They look happy," Marissa said, glancing over his shoulder. Rawlings and Rowan were making small circles on the floor, and she was laughing, no doubt at one of his famously bad but somehow still funny jokes.

"They are," Brandt said. "Just not as happy as us."

She laughed against his chest. "Are you always this confident?"

"Only when you're in my arms," he replied.

A few minutes later, the four of them gathered around a table with one wobbly leg. Brandt paid for beers for the rest of them, but stuck to soda for himself.

"Marissa," Rawlings asked, "is Brandt a distraction from your studies? I've always found him a little distracting," he added playfully.

Marissa shook her head. "Not at all. Believe it or not, Brandt is a great study buddy."

"I put her in hurry-up mode," Brandt joked, rolling his finger in a circular motion, "so we can get to the good stuff."

"Rawlings loves to play 'School,'" Rowan asserted, wrapping her arm around him. "Fill in the blanks on your own." He kissed her on the cheek.

"Just for that," he said in a low growl, "you've got detention all weekend."

"Promise?" she asked with a grin.

Marissa yawned and lifted one hand in apology. "Sorry about that, guys. I wasn't bored—I've just been burning the midnight oil lately."

"No need to apologize," Rowan assured her.

"You all ready to head home?" Brandt asked, his face neutral as they all nodded. "Let's go," he said, getting to his feet and helping Marissa up too. "I'll pick you up some milkshakes on the way home."

"My hero," she said, gripping his hand.

Brandt was true to his word—always, Marissa thought—and dragged them gladly through the nearest drive-through. When he dropped her off at her apartment, he stepped out of the truck to walk her up to her door. He lifted her chin, gave her a light kiss, then a more passionate one, the kind that sent heat rushing up her face.

"Get some rest," he commanded softly. "Gotta keep up your strength."

"That I do," she said, her hands resting atop his chest. "Goodnight, cowboy."

He laughed, kissed her softly one more time. "Goodnight, Miss Sloan."

As she watched them drive away, she suddenly remembered Rowan's earrings remained in her lobes. She smiled then, because it didn't matter—they'd all be together again soon enough.

• • •

"One hell of a night," Rawlings declared, half-dozing against the headrest. Brandt smiled—they were nearing home, and he was pretty sure his friend was buzzed, but they were both higher than the clouds when it came to emotions. Things had the feeling of falling into place, each of them settling into a happy routine that would only get better with time.

"You're in love," Brandt inferred, grinning as he stared out the windshield. "It's written all over your face."

"Aw, hell," Rawlings said, "can't a man love a woman and not have it be made into a federal crime?"

Brandt laughed. "How many did you have tonight, man?"

"I don't remember," he answered drowsily. "Five or six?"

"Closer to seven," Brandt murmured, "although I didn't keep close count. I just know I paid the tab."

"Much appreciated," Rawlings answered. Then he sighed. "So how do you really feel about Marissa and all of this fancy schooling?"

Brandt burst out laughing. "I'm supportive of everything she does," he asserted. "Why? Someone tell you different?"

"Maybe you're being honest with Marissa," he countered, "but I'm not sure you're being honest with yourself."

Brandt groaned almost inaudibly as the truck tires scooted up the driveway, beneath the oaks and maples and dogwoods. He pulled to a stop in his usual spot and shut off the engine, but didn't make a move to release his seatbelt or open the door. He leaned forward, resting his arms atop the steering wheel. "This might not make a whole lotta sense to you—or maybe you're the only one who'll get it—but I worry about my parents. Probably more than I should. If something happened to them, I'd be alone in the world."

"You'd have me," Rawlings said.

Brandt smiled. "I know. I'm just ready to settle down and have my own family. Maybe I wasn't ready a few months ago, but meeting her changed all of that. I know we can't have kids right away, but I would, at the very least, like to get married."

"Does Marissa know?"

He nodded. "I've told her as much, but I've still gotta buy a ring and ask the question."

"Do Mitch and Laura know?"

"They know too. I'm just not sure how serious they take me."

"I don't know about that, Brandt. When was the last time they tried to talk you out of anything?"

"Hmm." He pondered on it for a minute or two, and came up with only one memory. "They tried to talk me out of buying that car," he recalled.

"The one you broke your leg in."

"That's the one," he said, making a clicking sound with his cheek. "And I'm sure there were other things—plenty of them—they should've warned me about, but they figured I needed to learn from my mistakes." He leaned back and unfastened his seatbelt. "Do you need any help getting to your bed?" he asked, turning his attention to his friend. Rawlings shook his head in response.

"I'll be fine, man. Go on in and get some shuteye."

Brandt nodded, and they stepped out of the truck together. He followed his friend anyway, thinking there was something left unsaid—but damn if he could remember what it was. He was interrupted by a buzzing noise.

"That's my phone," Rawlings said, fumbling for the thing in his shirt pocket. "It's Brady," he added, his eyes sweeping over the screen. "My brother." In the fading light, Brandt saw a look of worry flash across his friend's face. He answered the phone, his voice remaining dispassionate throughout the conversation. Brandt kept one eye on him, and another somewhere off to the side—he already felt guilty about eavesdropping. "Okay," Rawlings said into the phone. "I'll think about it. Bye."

"Everything alright?" Brandt asked calmly as the phone was slipped back into Rawlings's pocket. As soon as their eyes met, instinct told him that things, indeed, weren't alright.

"My dad had a massive heart attack," he answered, his happy demeanor deflating like a balloon with a slow leak.

"My God," Brandt answered, stunned. "Is he..."

"He's in critical condition," Rawlings informed him, "but he's stabilized." His gaze lowered to the ground. "What should I do? Should I go?"

"I'll take you to the hospital, if you want to go," Brandt said. "I don't think you should be driving under the circumstances."

"Thanks," Rawlings said, giving him a tight smile of gratitude. Then he laughed uneasily. "I'd better change clothes first. I smell like a brewery."

Brandt nodded. "I'll be in the truck whenever you're ready." He watched his friend disappear inside the bunkhouse, and felt his heart clench. McCoy had already had enough heartache and misery to last a lifetime—going to the hospital to see a man who never gave him so much as an "I love you" showed a lot of grit and courage on his part. Climbing back into the truck Brandt suddenly envied his friend. He wished he could be that strong.

Chapter Seventeen

Brandt balanced the cup of decaf coffee between his thumbs, and listened to the cold, clinical sounds of the hospital. He was alone in the waiting room, accompanied only by his thoughts. He'd rousted his parents out of bed with his phone call, but they'd thanked him not only for letting them know but also accompanying his best friend on a difficult journey. His ears perked up as footsteps echoed down the hallway, and a moment later Rowan entered the waiting area. He stood and gave her a friendly hug. Her face carried a look of great concern.

"Thanks for coming," he said. "I wasn't sure if you were safe to drive."

"I didn't have as many he did," she reminded him. "I've always had a pretty good tolerance for beer. Liquor, on the other hand… sorry, I'm rambling. You brought him?"

Brandt nodded. "Even if he'd been sober, I still don't think it's a drive he should've made on his own. Too much raw emotion to think clearly."

Rowan nodded in agreement. "We've talked about his family but Rawlings is pretty guarded when it comes to personal stuff. Not his emotions—I mean, I know he loves me—but he puts up a veneer and I find myself wanting to know more."

Brandt glanced around to make sure no one else was in earshot. There were no secrets in a small town, but he had the good sense not to carelessly spread others' personal business. "The McCoys aren't the worst kind of parents you could have—one glance at the evening news will tell you that much—but they didn't give their kids much in the way of love or care. Rawlings spent countless nights at my house when we were growing up. My parents never cared—but then again, neither did his."

"One less mouth to feed," Rowan surmised.

Brandt shrugged. "Something like that." He smiled. "I'm glad he's found you. You've brought out the better parts of his personality, the parts he keeps hidden from everyone but me."

"He's such a good man," Rowan replied, a sad expression touching her lips. "You'd never know he came from such a sad background. Maybe I oughta thank your parents for that, though."

He shrugged again. "Maybe."

"You're a good influence on him, Brandt."

He was about to answer that when Rawlings half-stumbled through the doors. He went to Rowan and pulled her into a tight hug. It was easy for Brandt to see the red rimming his eyes as their gazes met for a split-second. "How is he?" she asked worriedly, easily gauging her boyfriend's anxiety.

"He needs open-heart surgery," Rawlings told them. "They're going to cut him open like a damned cow at the slaughterhouse." His voice broke over the words but he fought to maintain his composure. "I don't know what to do."

Rowan's hand massaged his back in soothing circles. "I'm here," she said. "I'll be with you the whole time."

He smiled. "Thank you, honey." His eyes drifted back to Brandt. "The ranch…"

Brandt gave him a small smile. How could he be thinking about the ranch at a time like this? Simple—his devotion to it. "I'll take care of everything, man. Don't worry about that—just take care of things on this end." He paused for a moment—the hospital was otherwise silent. It was after midnight. "Is your brother still here?"

He shook his head. "He wanted to get back to his wife and kid—hates to leave them alone."

"Your mom is still back there?"

He nodded. "She won't leave his side."

"Any of your sisters here?"

"Not a one of them showed up," Rawlings said with obvious disgust. "Can't say as I blame them, but Brady made the effort to call. That's more than they would've done had the situation been reversed."

"Do you need anything to eat?" Rowan asked, her eyes not leaving his face.

"Sure," Rawlings said, smiling tenderly at her. "And some coffee."

She nodded, then angled her gaze toward him. "Brandt?"

"I'm fine," he said. She was out of the room before he spoke again. "You want me to spend the night here?"

"Nah," he answered, shaking his head. "Thanks for bringing me. If I need to drop by and pick up some fresh clothes, I'll have Rowan drive me."

Brandt nodded. "You're welcome. I know it'll be a long night, but try to catch a few winks if you can. It won't do your dad any good for you to get run down too."

"I know," he said. "You're a hard taskmaster, you know that?" He laughed miserably, and a single tear slid down his tanned cheek.

"Everything is gonna work out," Brandt assured him. "Hey—I've never steered you wrong before, have I?"

"Only when beer was involved," Rawlings said, and they both laughed. They said their goodbyes and Brandt walked silently from the hospital, out into the humid evening air. He glanced up at the stars, praying for a miracle—maybe two or three. He was out of practice.

• • •

Marissa removed the lid from the cup of coffee Brandt had brought for her and took a sip. It tasted like tar, but she wasn't one to look a gift horse in the mouth. Brandt was seated on her couch, one wrist across his forehead as he guzzled from his own cup. It wasn't decaf, either.

"Tell me again why you didn't call last night," she said, planting herself beside him and crossing her legs together.

"Because," he said, smiling, "there's nothing you could have done, and you need your rest."

She traced the outline of his ear, knowing that it drove him crazy. "You treat me like a child sometimes, Brandt." A smirk lifted the edges of his mouth. "I'm pretty sure I can balance out college, work, and a personal life."

"I know, sweetheart," he said, removing his wrist from his forehead and taking her fingers in his. "Rowan was there, though, and I know Rawlings wouldn't have wanted us all underfoot, badgering him about his feelings."

Marissa nodded, knowing he was right. He usually was. "Did you talk to him this morning?"

"Briefly. I think they're going to do the surgery sooner rather than later. His mom turned into a hysterical mess so it fell to Rawlings and Brady to make the final decisions."

"I can't imagine the amount of stress he's under."

"Me neither, ma'am. I'm just glad he's got someone by his side."

"It definitely helps," Marissa said. Her breath caught in her throat when he turned his face toward hers, giving her his full attention. His words were confident, but in his eyes lurked grave concern. "A problem shared is a problem halved."

"Sometimes it's hard to believe that I ever lived without you." He smiled at her, the moment rife with meaning. "I didn't interrupt your studying, did I?"

"Coffee is never an interruption," she said, squeezing his hand, and they both laughed. "I was working on my midterm. I'm nearly done."

"Need me to proofread?"

"Only if you want to die of boredom," she joked, "and I'd rather you didn't do that just yet."

"Same here," he said, lifting his brows. "How's work going?"

"Pretty good," Marissa said, drinking the last of her coffee. "I still haven't told Mona that I might be leaving her at the end of the summer."

"Don't," Brandt cautioned. "Don't tell her until you absolutely have to."

"There you go again," she said, laughing, "scolding me and such."

His grin turned devilish. "You'd rather me turn you over my knee?"

"Ouch," she said, her grin reflecting his. "Well, not before the honeymoon." She grabbed their empty cups and tossed them in the trash, then headed for her desk again.

"I'd probably better get outta here," Brandt said from the corner of his mouth, "and let you get back to your work."

"Don't you dare," she said, pointing her finger at him. He'd already gotten to his feet and was halfway between her and the front door. "I have a better idea."

He grinned at her, his fingers hooked in his pockets. "And what might that be?"

"Give me enough time to finish this midterm…"

"I don't wanna rush you."

"I told you I was nearly done."

He gave her a sheepish grin. "So you did."

She flipped through her notes and brought the computer to life. "I want to spend the entire day with you, Brandt."

His forehead wrinkled at her assertion. "It's just gonna be ranch work, sweetheart. Nothing to get excited about."

"Will you be there?"

"Sure will," he said, laughing.

She gave him her most shameless grin. "That's all the excitement I need." And even though she never once met his gaze for the next thirty minutes, the computer her sole focus, she knew he smiled the entire time.

...

"Is it full yet?"

Marissa glanced at the water tank and nodded. "It's full."

He turned off the spigot, then stood and faced her. "Damn glad I bought you this thing," he declared, thumbing up the brim of her hat. "You look good in it."

"You rascal," she said, kissing him on the cheek.

"Proud of it. Now climb in the truck, ma'am, because we've got cattle to water." He made sure the tank was sealed, checked for debris around the truck—spring storms tossed branches everywhere, and Rawlings was otherwise occupied—and climbed behind the wheel. His gaze lingered on Marissa just long enough for her to notice, and he tore his eyes away when she smiled back at him. His mind was half-full of licentious thoughts, and they were alone on the ranch, but the animals were counting on him. They were nearing the edge of the ranch when he lifted a finger and tapped his forehead. "Remind me to check the garden when we get back," he said absently. "I'm pretty sure it doesn't need to be watered, but that's kind of my job to remember random stuff like that."

"You're a good kid," Marissa said. "I used to try to help my mom, but she's proud of her independence and wanted to teach me to be similar."

"At least she didn't teach you to hate all men," he mused. "That wouldn't have been good for either of us." He glanced toward her and was rewarded with a wink. He looked out the window at the trees and grass—today, nature and all its beauty bored him. "How long till you know your grade?" he asked.

"Before Friday," she replied. "It's kind of weird to study with a professor and never meet them."

Brandt laughed. "Some of the ones I had, I would've preferred to never meet."

"I hope you don't take offense," she said, "but there's this part of me that still can't imagine you as a college student."

"None taken, beautiful. And yeah, I was not your typical college student. I didn't hate city living, but I missed being able to see the stars in the sky at night."

"What is it about you and stars?" Marissa wondered aloud. Brandt's eyes drunk her in—plaid shirt, faded jeans, white Stetson, and tall boots—did she even have to ask? Wasn't it obvious from every look he gave her?

He narrowed his eyes thoughtfully and brought the truck to a halt. He leaned over, one arm resting along her seat, and smiled. "Stars are what I've always wished on," he reminded her. "Whether I wanted a new toy, or a good score on a math test, or just to get laid," he said, his neck turning crimson, "I always wished on a star. I didn't know any better then, and even though I now know you've got to make your own luck, I still wish on them. Not as much these days, though."

"Really?" she asked.

He reached out and stroked the ends of her blonde hair. "Nope. I'm pretty happy."

Her smile seemed to light her from the inside out. "Me too, Brandt. Me too."

After tending the cattle, then checking on the one in the barn and all of the chickens for good measure, Brandt showed Marissa the proper way to weed out a garden. When she told him it was backbreaking work, he just laughed and admired the sheen of sweat on her face. With the feeding and weeding out of the way, they headed into the house for a late lunch. When Marisa offered to help, Brandt brushed her aside. "After all," he said, "you're a guest in my home."

"Can I check out your room since I'm being shunned in the kitchen?" she joked.

"Sure thing," he said. "Take a right at the top of the stairs. It's the room with all of the cowboy hats."

He continued his work in silence, hoping that there was nothing too embarrassing lying around in his room. He was pretty sure his clothes were stowed in either the closet or the hamper. He'd made his bed—sort of. He'd probably vacuumed in there sometime in the previous month.

"Dammit," he muttered to himself, remembering the one childhood artifact still atop his dresser. As eagle-eyed as Marissa was, she'd notice it in a heartbeat. He heard her footsteps echo down the stairs and down through the hall, and waited for the ribbing to begin.

"Your room was surprisingly clean," Marissa said as she pushed through the door. "I knew you weren't a slob, but you're almost as OCD about clean as I am."

"You caught me on a good day," Brandt assured her. "There are times when I can't get the closet door shut because there's nothing but a mountain of dirty clothes in there."

"Hmm," she said, returning to her seat at the table. "I'd have to see that to believe it."

"That'll be your room too, when we get married." He cleared his throat. "Actually, that's not true. We'll take Mom and Dad's room."

"And where will they live?" she asked curiously.

"Dad has been talking about building a cabin," he said, tossing their lunch onto two plates. "Nothing fancy. We're talking two or three rooms at the most. Mom is looking forward to having a much smaller house to clean."

"I'd feel bad about pushing Mitchell and Laura out of their house," she said, her eyes widening as Brandt set the plate in front of her. She picked up her fork to eat, then paused to wait for him.

"Don't," he said, removing his hat and hanging it on the back of one of the empty chairs. "That's been the plan all along." They both dug into fried mushrooms, mashed potatoes, and scratch gravy. "There's no time limit on it, though. My parents never told me I had to be married by a certain date."

"This ranch is a wedding present," Marissa deduced after a few minutes of silence.

"Sort of," Brandt countered. "Except no one is leaving the ranch. My parents will build their cabin here, and I want Rawlings to stay around for as long as he'd like."

"It'll be a nice place to raise kids," she said, smiling. He nodded back at her, then resumed eating. "Brandt?" He looked at her expectantly.

"Hmm?"

"I saw the teddy bear in your room." He lowered his eyes, shook his head in humiliation. "Don't be embarrassed," she urged. "That thing is adorable—the straw hat, the overalls—I'm glad you kept it."

One eyebrow lifted. "And why is that?"

She smiled. "It gives me that much more insight into you, your childhood, and the man you are today."

All he could do was smile at her kind, thoughtful words. "Creaks and squeaks aside, this is a great house to grow up in." They finished eating, and he cleaned up the table. "Did you have fun today?"

"I did," she said. "A lot of hard work, but very rewarding. I look forward to it, you know."

He put the dirty dishes in the sink and began to run water for them. "To what?"

Marissa crossed the room and fell into his arms. She nestled gently into his neck. "To being carried up those stairs and making love to you," she said. "In our bed."

He felt the soft weight of her body, and the hefty weight of her words. "Me too, beautiful," he said, his throat raw, his voice hoarse. "Me too."

Chapter Eighteen

"I know it's poor etiquette to tell someone they look tired…" Josie said nervously.

"But I look tired?" Marissa answered. She yawned, trying in vain to cover her mouth as she did it. "I am." She sorted through a few misplaced items, organizing the counter in her habitual way. "Brandt practically dragged me out of that hospital when the surgery was over. Rawlings's dad made it through okay, and both men thought I should rest. I don't know whether to be flattered or insulted," she said with a sigh.

"I think it's okay to be both," Josie observed. "What woman doesn't want a man who is always looking out for her best interests, and vice versa?"

Marissa nodded. "There's some truth to that."

Josie smiled. "How is your class going?"

"Disturbingly well," Marissa replied, "and I have no complaints. It's like my undergraduate work, with all of its stress and worry, is a distant memory."

"I'm glad to hear it," Josie said, "although I am going to miss you around here."

"I'll miss you too, but I'll be…around. Thanks to Brandt, I've found a home here."

Josie turned toward the opening front door. "Speak of the devil," she said. Marissa turned and saw Brandt as well, and a brief smile passed between them.

"Good morning, ladies," he said with a nod as he strolled passed them and disappeared into another aisle. Marissa heard him whistling a tune briefly, the sound carrying across the store, and she stifled a laugh. He returned a minute later carrying a new pair of work gloves, and he laid them on the counter. "I wore out the fingers in my other pair," he said, taking out his wallet. "Hey there, Josie."

"Hi, Brandt," she answered. "I can give you two some privacy…"

"That won't be necessary," he said, raising a hand to stop her. His eyes drifted toward Marissa as they exchanged money. "I'm on my way to the hospital, but I wanted to stop and check on you first."

Marissa shook her head. "I'm fine, cowboy. I only laid awake half the night, but I still got more sleep than the average college student." She handed him the receipt. "Do you need me to bag your purchase today, sir?"

He laughed. "No, no, I think I'll just take them as-is." He tipped down the brim of his hat and picked up the gloves and receipt. "Don't work too hard, ladies."

"Bye, Brandt," Marissa said, and he pushed through the front door with his hip, turning back to grant her one last smile before he hit the parking lot.

"That man deserves some kind of acting award," Josie said a moment later.

Marissa feigned ignorance, but it was betrayed by the smirk on her face. "What do you mean?"

Josie rolled her eyes in a friendly manner. "You two have been involved for, I don't know, coming up on two months, and when he's in this store, around you, he's a perfect gentleman."

"Contrary to popular opinion," Marissa stated flatly, her eyes directed toward the back of the store, "Brandt is a gentleman."

"Even behind closed doors?"

Marissa laughed. "I relax my standards then."

They heard the office door open, and each of them resumed their standard positions behind the counter. Mona stopped near the register, and shot them a curious look, the kind a person gets when they know they've stepped into the middle of an inside joke. "You both remembered this is inventory day," she surmised. "I need you to stay late and make a checklist of what's in the storeroom as you clean it."

"Yes, ma'am," they said almost in unison.

"Good," she replied with a nod. "You seem to have an inherent knowledge of this store, as though you've worked here as long as I have. A valuable commodity to have in a pair of employees."

They both nodded, not saying another word as they waited for her to leave. "She just made my skin crawl," Josie announced. "If I didn't know any better, I'd think she had this place bugged and was secretly listening to our conversations."

Marissa frowned. It was no one's business who she dated, especially Mona's, but if she discovered the truth—and in a small town, she would sooner rather than later—she could make things harder on Marissa. And as much as she loved Brandt, that was a complication she didn't need.

•••

Brandt left his truck in the parking garage and took the elevator down into the hospital. The place was always busier than he thought it should've been, but a small farm town had more than its share of sickness and injuries. He made his way to the coffee shop, and scanned the area until he found Rawlings. He was tucked into a two-person booth, his brown eyes the same color as the coffee balanced between his hands. He looked up, gave Brandt a once-over as he slid into the booth.

"You want anything?" he asked in a ragged voice. "It's on me."

Brandt shook his head. "I'm fine. How's your dad?"

"Better." Rawlings let out a huge breath, but his shoulders remained taut. "That's what I wanted to talk to you about, Conner. I'm not coming back to the ranch for a while, maybe a month or two."

Brandt allowed his words time to sink in. Rawlings had done the bulk of the ranch work over the past seven years, a constant presence who kept the strain from building up between Brandt and his father—he was, in reality, each of their right hands. Brandt had known for a while that this day was coming, even before the heart attack. Life was changing, and he was unprepared to handle its rapid pace even as he mapped out his own future.

"I understand," he said.

Rawlings tried for a smile and failed. "Do you? It's going to be a long, hard recovery for him."

"It's going to be hard for both of you," Brandt guessed. "You've seen each other a handful of times since you left home, and now you're planning to move back under his roof."

He nodded. "I know." He took a drink of coffee, grimaced, and cleared his throat. "I'll miss y'all, but you'll understand it if I can't come around as much?"

"Sure," Brandt said, giving him a terse smile.

"Try to take care of the place for me."

Brandt nodded again. "I'll try. I can't make promises right now."

"Rowan and I are still together, it's just going to be a struggle to find time to date. My parents seem to like her, though."

"Good."

"Are you and Marissa okay?" he asked.

"We're great," Brandt assured him. "Every day is better than the one before."

"Good," Rawlings said. "Make sure you hang onto her, Brandt. You'll never be as happy alone as you are with her." Brandt nodded and was getting ready to confirm that assertion when Rawlings looked up at the clock on the wall. "I hate to break this up but we've got a shitload of information to listen to; the doctor is going to talk our ears off with all kinds of recovery stuff, dietary and activity guidelines, all that junk. I'll see you around, Brandt. Take it easy."

Brandt stood and shook hands with him. He felt like he was sending his best friend off to the battlefield—and in a way, maybe he was. "Good luck, man."

Rawlings laughed. "Same to you, man. I've got the feeling we're both going to need it."

Their hands broke apart and Brandt watched him walk away, his gait slow and steady, Rawlings in no particular hurry to settle into his new routine. Brandt sighed—he wasn't ready for it, either—any of it.

●●●

Brandt could tell something was wrong as soon as he arrived home. He stepped from the truck, and every hair on the back of his neck stood up. His father's truck was the only other vehicle parked in the yard; his mother must've been gone to town. He looked around—the leaves were still on the trees, with not a whit of wind in the air.

The noise filled his ears then, the sound of pain deafening. He ran toward the barn, toward the sound of the heifer crying, accompanied by the bawling of a calf. "Brandt!" his father cried in a strangled voice. His boots turned into bolts of lightning as he sailed through the barn door. Mitchell was in the stall with the cow, and her calf was half-out, clearly distressed. The two men's eyes met. There was no time to call a vet, or to scrounge for a pair of gloves. "Help me, son," Mitchell said, trying to simultaneously calm down the animals and prevent himself from being kicked.

Brandt sprinted into action, putting himself directly in the line of fire. He shoved a hand in the cow's hindquarters, on either side of her calf. The white animal, its fur matted, looked up at him with those big black eyes, almost as though it was saying, "Help me, I'm almost out."

The bawling and crying continued unabated. It was a struggle to step back and forth with the cow as she tried to give birth, and her skin was slicked with sweat. His boots slipped in the hay and manure, a smell that was both sweet and disgusting, but he maintained his footing.

"You've done this before," Mitchell reminded him through clenched teeth, his own foothold slipping. "And in worse weather."

That much was true, Brandt thought ruefully—whether the hottest heat of summer or the bitterly cold climes of winter when your breath froze as soon as it left your mouth, he'd taken care of cattle in both. And he'd suddenly grown sick of it.

"Come on, little guy," Brandt said, sweat pouring down his face and neck. He pulled hard enough to gain some leverage, but gently enough not to scare the animal, and finally he broke free. Brandt fell on his ass, the animal squarely placed in his lap. He took a deep breath, and saw relief cross his father's face as he leaned against the stall.

"Good job, son," Mitchell said. He slapped the cow lightly on one side. "You nearly gave me a heart attack, you damned cow."

Brandt nodded, and helped the calf to its feet. "You'd never know the poor thing was in distress," he said, hitching his chin toward it. Brandt stood up and shook his head—he was covered in blood and mucus from his chest to his boots.

"Go in the house and get cleaned up," Mitchell said, giving his son a bemused expression.

"You sure?" Brandt asked, wiping at his brow.

"Yeah, we'll be alright. You did good, son. Real good."

Brandt sighed as he fled the barn, giving the happy calf one last cursory look. Soon enough the thing would be nursing. He smiled to himself, thinking that his father's compliment was about as much praise as he was ever going to get from the old man. If he wanted something more, well, he'd have to look elsewhere.

• • •

"Heard you had some excitement today."

Brandt stacked the last of the dishes in the drainer and emptied the sink of water. "You could say that," he said impassively. He turned toward his mother and smiled. "I just did what had to be done."

Laura wiped her hands on a dishtowel and shook her head. "I hate that your father was out here alone," she told him. "I planned to run a quick errand but it ended up lasting much longer."

"It's gonna be different now, without Rawlings. He was the glue that held this ranch together."

At that moment, Mitchell walked into the kitchen, eyes firmly trained on his son. "Brandt, we need to talk," he began.

Brandt squared his shoulders. "I'm listening."

"You weren't here today when I needed you."

"Really, Dad?" He arched his eyebrows. "Not only was I here, I also delivered that calf by hand. He's healthy, by the way. I just checked on him before supper."

"That's not what I meant."

Laura stepped forward, placing an insubstantial barrier between two men whose body language spoke far louder than their words. Hackles up, jaws clenched—they might just as well have been two animals fighting over a meal.

"Where were you today, Brandt?" Mitchell asked sharply. "Why'd it take you so long to get home?"

"I stopped off to by a new pair of work gloves and check on Marissa. Then I went to the hospital and had a brief talk with Rawlings. I guess he shared the bad news with you already."

Mitchell nodded gravely. "He told me in person, and I gave him my blessing. But that's exactly what I'm trying to tell you—I'm gonna need your help now, more than ever, with McCoy gone."

Years of pent-up frustrations and remembered slights—real or imagined—boiled inside of Brandt like lava in a volcano, his skin and ears burning red. He slapped the counter with the heel of his palm, and Laura flinched. "That's what this is really about, huh, Dad? I was never enough for you. I was the kid you were stuck with, and I walked through fire to make you proud. I learned everything I could about this ranch, hoping you wouldn't make me go off to college and miss four years' worth of hands-on training. But then Rawlings, the default son, showed up and you could've cared less about me. How is it, Dad? If I left and never came back, you wouldn't care. You'd be fine."

"That's a lie, Brandt, and you know it," Mitchell shot back. "This ranch has always been and always will be your home. You're just not committed to it because you know it's yours already. Maybe if you'd stop being an ungrateful piece of hell, you'd be able to open your eyes to the truth."

"I'm out of here," Brandt said in disgust. His mother made a move to stop him, but he brushed past her without a word. Mitchell grabbed him by the arm on his way out of the kitchen. He tried to squirm away, but his father's hold was vise-tight around his bicep.

"Go ahead and resent me if you want to," he whispered. "I figure you've earned the right. But don't resent your best friend. He didn't have any of the advantages growing up that you did. You may not have been born with a silver spoon in your mouth, but you wanted for nothing. Nothing," he emphasized. "Just remember that when you're sitting around, feeling sorry for yourself."

When his fingers let go, Brandt raced out of the kitchen and up to his room. He searched for a duffel bag, then filled it with everything he could jam inside. He glanced at the interior of his room, muttered a few expletives, and tromped loudly down the stairs. His father was nowhere to be seen, but his mother waited for him at the end of the banister. Her eyes were glassy with tears.

"Brandt, he didn't mean it," Laura said. "You both said things you shouldn't have in the heat of the moment, and when you cool off you'll see that an apology is in order."

"I'm sick of apologizing, Mom. Let him see how easy it is to run this ranch by himself for a while."

Laura shook her head. She lifted her right hand, nearly brushing his cheek before she withdrew it. "You're an adult. I can't tell you what to do." She sighed. "I never could."

"You knew this day would come, Mom." Brandt slung the bag over his shoulder and gave her a quick kiss on the cheek. "I'll see you around. I won't go far."

He turned away from her then. As he headed out the front door, he recalled the teardrops on her face, and each one sliced through his heart like small daggers.

• • •

Marissa was reviewing her course notes when Brandt's knock came at the door. He'd called her from the end of his driveway, apprised her of the situation. She wasn't happy about it, but what could she do? She'd known Brandt was stubborn almost from day one. Hell, she was too. You had to be stubborn, she figured, to survive this thing called life.

She opened the door to find the saddest looking guy in history. Brandt's eyes were downcast, and it was the most miserable she'd ever seen him. He sighed, and frowned. She greeted him with a tight smile, hoping to assuage his feelings.

"Tell me I didn't make a huge mistake," he implored her.

She reached for his hand, massaged his strong, able fingers with hers. "I can't lie to you," she said, "but I can give you a place to stay. Come on in." He nodded at her, and as she closed the door behind him, she noted that he carried the duffel bag like it was full of bricks. He disappeared into the bedroom, and she simply shook her head.

Cohabitation had not been part of her plans.

Chapter Nineteen

Living with Brandt did have its advantages, however.

For the first time Marissa was able to fall asleep in his arms, and wake up in the same position, cradled next to his heart. Sometimes he'd stroke her awake with his scratchy, brown stubble, laughing as he roughed her up. She had to admit that it felt pretty damned good. Finding him half-naked in her kitchen, cooking breakfast, was no hardship either. But for all of the obvious physical benefits, she had known from the beginning that it was wrong. She and Brandt were meant to start their lives together under the roof of their own home, not in the upstairs apartment of a feed store.

Broaching the subject with him had been unsuccessful, primarily because she couldn't get past his easy defense of his position. How do you tell a full-grown man that he needs to move back home, and in with his parents? Even the bunkhouse would've made more sense. As things stood now, Brandt was completely negligent in his duties regarding the ranch. To Marissa's knowledge, he hadn't set foot there in weeks.

Her first class came to an end, and they celebrated together when she earned an A. There was little time for leisure, though, because she began an eight-week course the very next Monday. Her nose was to the proverbial grindstone, and she had no clue how Brandt could so thoroughly enjoy watching her study. He cooked and cleaned, but she couldn't figure out how he enjoyed this new lifestyle—surely no self-respecting cowboy would be content to wash dishes and watch his girlfriend take quizzes?

She was returning from another long, draining eight-hour day in the store, and he greeted her with a kiss as soon as she cleared the threshold. Okay, she thought, another point in favor of him living here. He handed her a stack of mail, his face lighting up like a neon sign.

"Pretty sure there's good news in there," he told her as they took their seats on the couch.

Marissa immediately tossed aside several pieces of junk mail—how could you get on a mailing list so fast after moving somewhere? Then she rifled through until she found what Brandt had been so excited for her to open. Anxiety and joy threaded around her heart simultaneously. "This is it," she said, almost an aside.

"Open it, sweetheart." His arm drifted from the back of the couch and down around her shoulders.

She took a deep breath, swallowed, and slipped her thumbnail under the seal. She'd never been so nervous in all her life. She withdrew the letter, unfolded it, and read the words two or three times before she reacted.

"What does it say?" Brandt asked.

"I'm in," she told him, her voice dazed. She handed him the letter and he let out a whoop.

"Hot damn," he said, tossing it aside and scooping her into his arms. He got to his feet and danced around the room like *he* was the one who'd just received good news. He kissed her, his tongue sliding against hers and drawing a moan from her throat.

"You're not the tiniest bit upset?" she asked, stroking his face between her hands.

"Hell no," he replied. "This is great news."

"Brandt," she said carefully, looking deep into his eyes, "they're admitting me in August."

"Because they loved your essay," he reminded her. "They can see how smart you are. It's like I've been telling you all along—they'd be fools not to take you."

He kissed her again. "Brandt," she murmured against his lips. Eh, what the hell, she thought—let him have his way with me for now. He carried her to the bedroom, and for the next half-hour or so, her worries subsided.

But it was a temporary respite. As they dozed beneath the sheets afterward, she pressed herself to his back, holding him a little too tightly. "A man needs his rest," he said drowsily, his voice still hoarse. "Especially when he's with you."

She ran her palm across his stomach in an enticing manner, but moved no lower. "Brandt, we need to talk."

He exhaled sharply. "I recognize that tone of voice. Let me have it."

Marissa levered herself up just long enough to leave a kiss on his shoulder. "I'm giving up this apartment when I go off to college. Where are you going to live then?"

"Maybe I'll go with you," he said, grabbing her hand and clutching it beneath his, near his heart. "I've got a degree myself— surely I could find something."

She felt incredibly fragile inside—for the first time in their relationship, Brandt was content to stare at the wall as they spoke, his eyes cast away from her. It was an unwelcome change. "You'd never be happy, Brandt. You are not made to live in the city."

"Dammit, Marissa," he ground out between his teeth. "I don't need you to tell me who I am or what I feel. Isn't that what we've built this thing on—unconditional love and all that crap? Have I ever tried to force anything on you?"

"No…" she said.

He quickly cut her off. "Then why are you making such a big deal about this? Haven't I been helping you pay rent?"

"Yes, you have," she said pointedly. "And you're miserable. Oh, you might put on a brave face for the rest of the world, but you're forgetting that I know you better than anyone else in your life. You need…"

"What I need is to get out of this damned bed and fix supper," he said sharply. When he tried to move, she locked her arms around him until he changed his mind.

"Brandt?" she asked softly.

"Yeah?" he answered brusquely.

"I'm sorry."

He sighed. "I'm sorry too, sweetheart." He kissed her fingertips. "I love you too much to ever mean anything I say when we fight. I hope you know that."

"I do," she said, her cheek pressed against his shoulder. As genuine as she thought his words sounded, she would've given anything, in that moment, for just one loving gaze from his eyes.

But it never came.

• • •

"How did we get here, Rowan?" Marissa asked, in between bites of her sandwich. In truth, her appetite was minimal these days. Guilt had rendered her stomach useless. Brandt had told her he was heading out to run some errands—she hoped that's what he was doing, anyway—and she met with Rowan for their usual Saturday time-wasters. "Everything I say and do feels wrong these days."

Rowan nodded. "How is school going?"

"Fine, actually. That's the only part of my life that doesn't feel like a train wreck."

Rowan laughed. "Yeah, that part with the good-looking guy under your roof, waiting on you hand and foot, sounds just awful." But her smile was sympathetic. "Rawlings told me they've stopped speaking."

That much was true, Marissa thought ruefully—Brandt had long-since stopped checking his phone for incoming calls or text messages. "Everything is so messed up, Rowan. For years Brandt had only his parents and his best friend. Now he has only me. I really should've sent him back home that first night, but…"

"But what?" Rowan asked. "You loved him too much to turn him away?"

"That's about the size of it." Marissa forced some food into her mouth, was relieved when it willingly slid down her throat. Her stomach was certainly grateful. "Or maybe…could it be that he wanted this all along?"

Rowan shook her head. "Too many dominoes had to fall. None of us were expecting Mr. McCoy's heart surgery, or that Rawlings would move back home to help him convalesce. From what I've gathered, this is simply the product of years of resentments between father and son."

Marissa stirred her drink with an unused straw, then took a sip. "Even if I had grown up with my dad around, I guess I wouldn't be able to empathize. Father-son and father-daughter relationships are fundamentally different. I've witnessed some of the tension between Mitchell and Brandt, but I don't think it merits nearly the amount of bad feelings that Brandt seems to harbor."

"I count myself lucky that I've never had these kinds of parental issues," Rowan said, shaking her head. "I don't envy any of you."

"He may hate me for this," Marisa realized, "but I have to fix things for Brandt."

"I doubt he'll hate you," Rowan countered. "Just…tread lightly."

Marissa frowned. "That's the problem—I've been keeping my words reined in, when I should've been putting my foot down. Sorry," she apologized in advance, pulling out her phone. "I have to make a call."

Rowan smiled. "It's perfectly okay."

She dialed, put the phone to her ear. "Yes, this is Marissa. Could I meet with you tomorrow? I know it's short notice. Okay, great. That sounds great. I'll see you then. You too. Goodbye."

"Everything okay?" Rowan asked, lifting her eyebrows in a questioning manner.

"It will be," Marissa answered with a nod. "If not for me, then at least for him."

• • •

She wouldn't have been surprised if they'd barricaded the door against her.

Marissa knocked on the front door, glanced around at the ranch. The place was eerily quiet. The bunkhouse looked strangely forlorn, and even the chickens were silent in their roost. She wondered if this wasn't some sort of cosmic sign—things were out of balance, off-kilter, with no one in their usual place. She sighed, feeling somewhat relieved when Brandt's mother opened the door and greeted her with a smile.

"Come in," Laura said quickly, guiding her with a hand along her shoulder. "Mitchell is out on the ranch somewhere." They sat down in the living room, and Laura offered her something to eat or drink, which she politely turned down. "I'm glad you called," she told Marissa. "I'm also thankful for your updates."

"I'm so sorry, Laura," she said. "This is my fault."

"Nonsense," Laura argued. "This has been brewing for years. I just foolishly hoped things would never come to a head."

"They're too much alike," Marissa suggested tentatively. "That's been a common thread during our conversations."

"I wish it weren't true," Laura said, fingers knotted together nervously. "When Brandt stubbornly refused to eat his baby food, I knew exactly what I was dealing with. I'd seen it enough during my marriage. Don't let me persuade you otherwise—I love Mitchell and everything about our life together. He's a very caring man, and Brandt truly has no idea how much his father loves him."

"Is there a way…?" She stopped, and both women's eyes moved to the doorway, where another set of footsteps had joined them.

"Don't stop on my account, ladies," Mitchell declared, putting up both hands. "Proceed."

"Mitchell," Laura said with unusual severity, "Marissa came by today to help. I think you could do her the honor of listening to what she has to say." Instead of turning on his heel and walking back out, as Marissa expected, he nodded somberly and took a seat in his usual armchair.

"Mr. Conner, I was just telling your wife that I feel like this is somehow my fault. I gave Brandt an easy out, an escape, instead of forcing him to work out his problems."

Mitchell shook his head. "Young lady, our problems run bone-deep. I did my best, but maybe I was never the kind of father Brandt deserved. It's hard when your child is strong-willed. You know they'll be okay, but you don't know how to guide them."

"I think the opposite is probably true," Marissa said. "It was your guidance that made him strong-willed, kind, and upright. Maybe he's forgotten all of that and simply needs a reminder."

"Well, Marissa," he asked, "what did you have in mind?"

She lifted her chin and looked at each of them in turn. "I'm going to break his heart."

• • •

Mitchell and Laura worked to change her mind, but Marissa wouldn't be swayed. She would be leaving Layton in the rear-view mirror soon enough, and there was no point in tearing off the bandage slowly. It would hurt less if she did it now. Oh, it would still hurt—it would be like slicing off a piece of herself and letting the blood flow freely—but it was the only way to salvage Brandt's future. But, as Marissa reflected later, the best laid plans …

He was waiting for her, his stance casual as he lounged on her couch. His face belied something else, however, a harshness she wasn't used to seeing there. "Did you have a nice day?" he asked calmly.

She nodded. "It was very productive."

"Where did you go?"

She froze at his question, and then met his eyes. They were not a pleasant shade of green. "I went to visit your parents," she answered unemotionally.

"I followed you."

She nodded again. "Then you know I was there for quite a while."

"What did you talk about?" he asked, dodging her inquiry. "What a screw-up I am?"

The backs of her eyes stung with rage—or maybe sorrow. "I was apologizing to them for my mistakes," she said. "I was also saying goodbye."

His face fell. "Goodbye? What the hell do you mean?"

"I'll be leaving soon," she reminded him. "Graduate school. My big dream. The one you pushed me to pursue. Who knows where life will take me? Therefore, I wanted them to know how much I appreciated their hospitality and friendship, and the wonderful time I had spent with the man they raised. I told them I'd always treasure it."

He clenched his jaw tightly, his eyes now blazing with anger. "What did you do, Marissa? Dammit, what did you do?"

"I promised them I'd get you home, you stubborn fool!" Sobs tore at her voice until her throat was raw and aching. "If you don't have me to lean on, you'll have no other choice."

"How could you say that?" he screamed. "This is my life, dammit! Mine." He slammed a fist against his chest. "No one makes a decision for me—no one."

"Well, maybe they need to," she answered coldly. "You're not a child, Brandt. When you make a commitment, you have to stick to it."

"What about you?" he retorted. "What about us? I thought we were committed, Marissa. Was I just too stupid to see the difference?"

She laid down her purse and walked over to where he stood. His entire body was shaking with barely-concealed rage, and he was flushed red atop his tan. Marissa felt an odd stirring of sexual arousal then, her mind recalling how passionate and tender he could be anytime they were in bed. At that moment, she wanted nothing more than to hold him, to tell Brandt that everything would be okay.

"I still want to marry you," she whispered. "Maybe I always will. But it will be easier if we just get this out of the way now, before we get any more involved."

"More involved?" he said, his voice cracking. His whole face was pained, and she knew that tears were forthcoming. "We're living together. I love you so much that it literally hurts. You can't tell me you don't feel the same way."

"No, I can't," she agreed. "That would be a lie."

"Then tell me how to fix this," he begged her. "Tell me how to make things right."

She looked into his eyes, his gaze unwavering. She really hated herself right now. She couldn't remember ever putting this look of hurt on the face of another living soul. Maybe that's what love was, she thought—the power to hurt someone so deeply without ever meaning to.

"Go home, Brandt," she said firmly. "Go home."

He nodded simply, his eyes turning cold and sad. He started to touch her, then stopped, his hand shaking in regret. He picked up his keys from their place atop the counter, and hit the door running. He didn't look back, and neither did she. She just cursed herself up one side and down the other. She'd given him an ultimatum, played an unforgivable mind game. It was too late for regrets, she told herself—the die had been cast.

She fell to the couch and cried buckets, until she was sure her tear ducts would pump out only dust. So much for this being quick and painless, she thought regretfully.

•••

He'd been a damned fool.

Marissa's words were as right and true as anything he'd ever been told in his life. He'd just been too stubborn to acknowledge them, to pull her into his arms and make the hurt go away. *I really am stubborn*, he thought to himself. *Just like my father.*

That put the taste of bile in his mouth, and he sat up in the truck bed just in time to see Rawlings driving down the dirt road, edging along the creek bank. There'd been no guarantee he would show up, but Brandt was damned glad to see him. He parked alongside, climbed out, and met Brandt with hard eyes—it was a look that spoke volumes.

"I was hoping you'd come," Brandt said, smiling, but the expression was not reciprocated.

"You sounded miserable," Rawlings said, shrugging, "and you were always there for me when I had hard times. I needed to return the favor."

"Even though I don't deserve it." Brandt drummed his hands on the tailgate. Plenty of sons had issues with their fathers, but turning his back on his best friend, ignoring him for no good reason, had been a huge mistake on his part, a juvenile act of behavior that he was ashamed of.

"Exactly."

Brandt nodded. "How is your dad?" he asked, changing the subject.

Rawlings joined him on the tailgate, letting out a huge breath in the process. "I'd forgotten what an asshole he is." He laughed uneasily. "He's okay. Recovering as the doctors expected. Trying to eat better. Brady comes by when he can and gives the old man a piece of his mind. Did I ever tell you my brother can be kind of scary?" Brandt shook his head. "Really. He's got more spine than any of the rest of us ever thought about having."

"Don't be so hard on yourself," Brandt cautioned him. "You're a good man too."

"I asked Rowan to marry me," he blurted out. Brandt looked at him in pleasant surprise and smiled. "I didn't give her a ring yet, but I wanted her to know that I was ready for commitment at some point."

"Marissa wants to break up with me," Brandt admitted.

"No she doesn't," Rawlings asserted. "She just wants you to get your head out of your ass and be a man."

Brandt's mouth fell open. "Says who?"

"Says me, dammit!" Rawlings rapped his knuckles anxiously against the truck bed, then flung himself upright and made a few circuits up and down the shoreline. Brandt watched him, his features hidden by the late day shadows. Finally he stopped directly in front of him, looking like he couldn't decide whether to hug Brandt or punch his lights out. "She wants you to go home," he said.

"That's right," he answered with a nod. "I told you that much over the phone."

"Do you know what Marissa saw when she came to the ranch for the first time?" Brandt shook his head. "Same thing I did—a happy family, two people who loved their kid and thought he hung the moon."

"Rawlings, I…"

"Shut up and listen, Conner. If I started working on my relationship with my dad right now, we'd never have what you and

Mitch do—never. He's just not that kind of man. Mitch, on the other hand, gave you his time, patience, and love from the day you came squealing into his life." Rawlings looked toward the sunset and shook his head. "I always envied that, man. Maybe that's why I tried to poach from you all of these years. I wanted Mitch to be my dad too, and in a way I got that while you were gone." He cleared his throat, raw emotion evident in the movement of his neck muscles. "Mitch told me you helped deliver the calf."

Brandt sighed. "I did. And then I ran away and left him."

"No one ever said it would be easy," his friend reminded him. "You and your father are cut from the same cloth. Just think about what Laura has had to put up with all these years."

"Yeah," Brandt said, his face blank. "A lesser woman would've run screaming for the hills a long time ago."

Rawlings laughed. "You got that right." He shoved his hands in his pockets and shot his friend a hopeful look. "So now what?" he asked.

Brandt nodded. "I apologize. To you, first of all, for ignoring you the past month or so. You probably could've used a friend, and I was a coward."

"I forgive you," Rawlings said immediately. "That's what best buds do."

He smiled, narrowing his eyes against the sunlight. "Do you have any free time this week?"

"I can take some time tomorrow," he said. "Do you need me?"

"Yes," he answered, grinning. It was a look that Rawlings recognized, and soon he was grinning too. "I have plans. Big ones."

• • •

Marissa was taking a nap on the couch when the noise startled her awake. A key was turning in the lock. She sat upright as he pushed through the door. She must've looked like hell—red, swollen eyes, tear-stained cheeks—but when Brandt saw her, he smiled, that same familiar expression that spoke volumes about how he felt—how he would always feel for her. Her heart lifted and she ran into his arms, knocking his keys to the floor, his hat nearly falling off his head.

"Take it easy, sweetheart," he said, trailing kisses along her jawline.

"I'm sorry, Brandt," she said, taking in the smell, touch, and feel of him, and never wanting to let go. "I shouldn't have gone behind your back and then set out to hurt you."

"I'm the one who's sorry," he whispered. "Sorry for putting you in the middle, for squatting at your place without considering the consequences. I was a jerk."

"I did enjoy having you in my bed," she admitted. He laughed heartily.

"I liked that part too. Damn, you look good first thing in the morning."

She gripped his back even tighter. "Ditto."

He nudged her face back toward his, kissed her with his tongue, his lips, even his teeth, his entire mouth possessing hers. When she thought she'd pass out from the emotional rollercoaster of the day, he carried her to bed, undressing her and then himself. "And now, for my favorite part of fighting," he said, his chest resting on top of hers. His thumbs brushed across her mouth and chin, then his fingers parted her hair across the pillow. "Making up," he said hoarsely, his mouth coming down on hers again.

He made love to her slowly and gently, their bodies singing together, finding a new pinnacle, until they crashed headfirst into a long, exhilarating climax. He held her tight against him afterward, each touch of his fingertips sizzling on her skin. When she was nearly asleep, he slipped from beneath the covers, put his clothes back on, and began to pack his things.

"Brandt," she said sleepily. "Don't go."

He zipped the bag before he came and sat down on the mattress. She opened her eyes and looked up into his smile. "I have to go home," he reminded her. He kissed her softly, first on the forehead and then the mouth. "I have so much to do, so many things to get ready."

"Ready?" she echoed.

He smiled warmly, an expression she wanted to save and keep in her mind's eye for the rest of her life. "For our wedding," he said. "We're getting married before you start that Master's degree." She opened her mouth to speak, and he placed one finger atop her lips. "Get some rest, Marissa. You look so beautiful when you sleep."

Chapter Twenty

Mitchell welcomed his son home with open arms. Laura scolded him at first, gave him a piece of her mind until he was sure his backside was raw—but then she pulled him into a hug too, and he was relieved. He was incredibly lucky to have two loving parents, when so many people had either lost theirs or never had them at all. When Laura excused herself to the kitchen—she thought Brandt needed something to eat, even if it was nearly midnight—Mitchell pulled his son into a fierce hug, the kind Brandt hadn't felt since that day at the hospital when they put his leg in that cast.

"I missed you, son," he said over Brandt's shoulder. "I'm so damned proud of you. You have to know that."

"I know, Dad. It just took me about twenty-five years to realize your way of showing it is different than most. And, Dad?"

"Yeah, son?"

"I love you."

Mitchell laughed, the sound thick with a tangle of emotions. "I love you too, Brandt. No man ever had a better son."

Laura returned then, clearing her throat to announce her presence. The men separated, and she looked at them curiously. "Eat some of this chicken," she told Brandt, pushing the plate toward him. "You look skinny, almost frail." She left the room, muttering something about having to do laundry for two men again instead of one.

Mitchell laughed. "Welcome home, son. Believe me, you were sure missed around here."

"Thanks, Dad. And goodnight."

"Goodnight, Brandt." And with that, he was alone again with his thoughts. He ate quietly, then set the plate aside, got to his feet, and walked toward the window. The bunkhouse was dark, no light from its windows, and he shook his head. As much as he empathized with Mr. McCoy's plight, he'd have to get Rawlings back on the ranch sooner rather than later. There was no other solution that seemed amenable. For him to be happy, it had to be all or nothing. Was he being selfish? Maybe, he acknowledged—but he also wouldn't apologize for it.

He put the plate in the sink and climbed the stairs, yawning as he took one riser at a time. He left his duffel bag on the floor and collapsed onto the bed, barely getting his boots off before he passed out cold.

• • •

"Show us the ring again," Laura said, and Brandt handed her the box. She popped it open, letting the light from outside catch in the diamonds and sparkle across the kitchen.

"I'm going to ask her tonight," Brandt promised. "Rawlings helped pick out the ring."

"That boy has a good eye," Mitchell said. "And so do you."

Brandt smiled. "Thanks, Dad." Mitchell nodded. "Do you think this is too soon?"

"Not at all," Laura assured him. "There's no timetable for love."

"It'll take a little bit of doing," Mitchell figured. "Where did you two wanna have it?"

"We've talked about doing it here at the house," Brandt informed them.

"It would be beautiful on the front porch," Laura suggested. "I could cover the posts with flowers. It'll be small, just family and friends, and I'll do the cooking."

"Marissa will love that," Brandt said, smiling, happier than he'd ever been in his life. "But you'd better confer with her just in case."

"Of course! She's going to be my daughter now so I want to get things started on the right foot."

Mitchell laughed at his wife's unnecessary fretting. "It may have taken a little extra time, but we've finally got the houseful of kids we always wanted."

Brandt leaned off of the counter, went over to place a hand on his father's shoulder. "Brace yourself, Dad. We picked up two rings today…"

...

Marissa knew what was going on.

From the moment Brandt arrived at her door, he'd carried a gleam in his eye, like a luminescent tear that refused to fall from his dark lashes. They had plans for the evening, but first he drove her out to his favorite spot, the steam emerging from atop the water. It was a sultry, humid night, perfect for a quiet moment with a lover—or perhaps something more life altering.

He helped her onto the tailgate, his hands lingering just long enough on her hips to draw a blush. Or maybe that was just the heat—either way, it felt nice. He immediately dropped to the ground, and got down on one knee.

"Marissa Sloan, will you marry me?"

"Yes," was her immediate response. Somehow the ring was on her finger before she knew what was happening. He got to his feet and leaned into her kiss.

"Sorry for the lack of fireworks," he told her. "I wanted the big moment out of the way." He cleared his throat and looked into her eyes. "I was just a silly, spoiled kid when I met you, walking around inside a man's body. I was probably a little apathetic too, but you knocked me flat on my ass."

Marissa glanced down at the diamonds in the ring, crystal-clear and refracting light against her skin. Amazing. "I played hard-to-get," she reminded him. "Did it drive you crazy?"

Brandt laughed. "A little bit. I didn't expect any of this, but I'm damned glad it happened. You're the best part of me, Marissa. You show me every day what I can accomplish, what kind of man I can be. It's a powerful thing. I'm in awe of you, your ability to roll with the punches and get back up when life knocks you down."

"You drew all of that out of me, Brandt," she insisted, framing his face in her hands. "You showed me that I could rely on you, depend on you, even when I didn't need to. That meant the world to me, to know that you had my back. I fell in love with you so quickly, and when I met your family I fell even more deeply, because I could see where you'd come from, how life had shaped you into such a good man. I guess that's why I was so hard on you when you left home and moved into my place. I loved having you there."

He smiled, his expression one of unbridled confidence. "I'm pretty good in the kitchen."

"Yes, you are," she replied, her lips brushing over his mouth. "Which is going to come in handy when we're married and I'm working long hours to support us." They laughed together at her lighthearted assertion.

"Not even married yet and already giving orders," he said, shaking his head. "I love you, Marissa. I'm always going to love you."

He was staring deep into her eyes again, his eyes on the verge of watering. "I love you too, cowboy." She grinned. "Limp and all."

He laughed so loud then that it echoed down the still waters of the creek, beneath the shade trees and across the next pasture. It shrouded her the way that she knew his love always would, an emotion so strong it would endure across space and time. Their own children would know something she hadn't—a father's love.

He helped her from the truck bed, but didn't put her feet on the ground. He held her aloft, against him, so tight that she could feel his heart beating through his shirt. He gave her one of those meaningful looks just before he kissed her again, the kind where his feelings were evident even if he couldn't put them into words. "You ready?" he asked after a moment. It was a loaded question, but not hard to answer.

She wrapped her arms around him, squeezed until there was no space between them. His smile grew larger. "Yes," was all she said.

• • •

"A toast to the future," Brandt said, clinking their beer bottles together. He and Marissa were seated together, her hand on his thigh, and Rawlings and Rowan occupied the opposite side of the booth. Rowan had a diamond on her finger too, and everyone was smiling big tonight. It was an evening made for celebration.

"But not too many cheers," Marissa reminded them in a joking manner. "Some of us have work in the morning. And homework afterward."

"Count me amongst those people who don't miss college one bit," Rowan said, cocking her head sympathetically.

Rawlings tugged her closer to him. "But you've still got plenty to learn about being a rancher's wife," he pointed out, smiling.

Rowan and Marissa tapped their bottles together. "Here, here," Rowan said drily, then whispered something in Rawlings's ear. He laughed.

"What was that?" Brandt joked, hitching his chin toward them. "Inside joke?"

"I told him that I was picturing him with just his hat on," Rowan revealed.

"Fiery damned redhead," Rawlings said in obvious admiration.

"You two are going to be in our wedding?" Marissa asked hopefully.

"Hell yes," Rawlings told her. "Wild horses couldn't keep us away." They were finished with their food and waiting on the check when his eyes drifted to the side and he declared, "Here comes trouble."

Four pairs of eyes glanced in the same direction, as Britt Larkin strolled over to their table. She was wearing jeans that were too tight, a shirt that was too small, and hair color that was too blonde for her bloodline. In short, she was someone's dream—just not Brandt's.

"Well, well, well," she said, stopping close to the table. Brandt looked away from her in disgust. "I didn't know you two were dating."

"For quite a while now," Marissa affirmed before anyone else could join in. "We're very happy."

Britt gave them a sarcastic grin. "Interesting. Just a word of warning, honey?"

Brandt glanced at Marissa, and found her as cool as a cucumber. He smiled to himself. "And what might that be?" she asked, her eyebrows lifted in expectation.

"He's kind of a player," she educated them. "In fact, he wrote the book on being a player."

"I'll try to keep that in mind," Marisa replied coolly. "Anything else, Britt?"

She looked from side to side, and lowered her voice as though divulging the secret code for a missile silo. "I already had him, honey. He's not that good."

Marissa simply laughed, and put her face closer to Britt as she revealed her own secrets. "Sounds like that's something you need to work on, sweetie—because when he performs in my bed, there's usually an encore."

Britt turned on her heel then, scoffed a bit, and walked away. The wind had been taken from her sails, and she slinked back to her corner of the bar.

"And a standing ovation," Marissa told the table, and they all burst into laughter. "It's funny now," she said, "but word will get to Mona before you can blink an eye. That'll be a fun conversation."

"Forget her," Brandt said. He massaged her shoulder lovingly. "I'm proud of you, by the way. You handled her like a pro."

"That's nothing," Marissa countered, but her fragile smile said otherwise. "I've dealt with far worse—but few that were so badly dressed." She sighed, and Brandt recognized her expression—she slipped quickly into empathetic counselor mode. "I think she just needs someone to love her, the way that you love me—and the way that Rawlings and Rowan love one another." She picked up her beer, and shifted modes again. "Here's to all of us," she said, echoing Brandt's words from earlier. "And our very happy, but very busy futures."

That was something they could all toast to.

• • •

Marissa took a deep breath and knocked on the office door. "Come in," she heard Mona say, and she pushed through, closing the door behind her.

"We need to talk," she said. Mona nodded.

"Yes, we do."

"I was admitted to graduate school and I will be leaving you soon, sometime within the next month."

"Britt told me about your chance encounter," she announced, "not that she needed to. I've known for a while that you and Brandt were together, despite my warnings to you."

Marissa frowned, unsure of exactly how to react. She felt a measure of sympathy for Mona following her mother's big reveal of their past, but she couldn't imagine ever being friends with this woman. She was simply too cold and judgmental. "How did you know?" she worked up the nerve to ask.

"His truck was parked outside of your apartment for weeks and weeks. It wasn't hard to put two and two together." She leaned back in her chair and steepled her hands together like the villain in some old movie. "I could have fired you. I could have evicted you—technically you broke your lease by allowing someone to live with you without seeking prior permission."

Marissa squared her shoulders and stood up straight. "You wouldn't have done either of those things, Mrs. Larkin. It would have been very un-Christian of you."

"What would you know about being a Christian?" Mona retorted. "Not only were you living in sin, but your mother is divorced. Hardly a good example of godliness."

Marissa smiled and arched one eyebrow toward her employer. "Brandt and I are in love," she reported happily, "and last time I checked, that's about the most Christian thing a person can do." Mona remained silent, and she decided to get one last thing off her chest before she left the office that day. "I wanted to thank you for this opportunity. I have learned a lot about myself and others during my time here, and moving to Layton has been the greatest adventure of my life. I will always look back on these months with fond memories—they were truly the building blocks of my future."

Mona nodded, and gave her a faint smile. "You've been an exemplary employee, and have proven yourself to be a hard worker. You can stay here until you need to leave, and then I will wish you good luck in your future endeavors. I have a feeling you're going to succeed."

Marissa was touched. "That's very kind of you to say, ma'am. I didn't expect that."

The older woman made a motion toward Marissa's ring finger. "If that's what I think it is, then I'll hardly be getting rid of you. And as someone who has attended church with Laura Conner for many years, the last thing I want to do is to draw the ire of her future daughter-in-law. I only hope your marriage will be a happy one."

"Thank you, Mona," she said. "Thank you so much."

"You're welcome," Mona replied. "Now get back on the floor and help me move some seeds."

Marissa laughed. "With pleasure."

· · ·

The wedding came on a humid day in August, on a Saturday where everyone managed to put their lives on hold. It took place on the front porch, per Laura's suggestion, with their regular minister officiating. Rawlings and Rowan were the best man and maid of honor, so polished and put-together that it looked like a dry run for their own upcoming nuptials. Mitchell and Laura witnessed the event, along with Josie, and Connie gave her daughter away. Marissa's father had responded to his wedding invitation with a handwritten letter—and for Marissa that had been enough. He wished that she have a bright future and everything he was never able to give her. She may never know her father, she acknowledged, but she wasn't the one to blame for his absence. Besides, she would now have Mitchell, who was warm in personality and generous with his time and wisdom.

They spoke their vows carefully—Brandt in a navy suit and blue-striped tie, his hair gelled and combed into place by his father; Marissa in a fitted white dress, holding a bouquet made up of wildflowers. They'd squeezed a whole lot of time and learning about one another into a few short months, and they weren't done yet. When they slid the rings onto their ring fingers, their eyes locked together, it was a binding promise that they'd spend a lifetime together. It was going to be an odd, unconventional marriage at first—but as far as they were concerned, that suited them just fine. Being married was the important part.

•••

They sealed their union with a prayer, a kiss, and a whole lot of dreams. Somehow, Brandt vowed to himself, he'd make sure they all came true. They'd just finished cutting the cake—Laura had done an amazing job with the spread, better than any caterer could have on such short notice—and shoving it into each other's mouths, when Connie stepped up behind her son-in-law and pulled him into a hug. "You are," she said, dabbing at her eyes, "the finest man I could have ever picked for my daughter."

"You raised a fine daughter, Connie," he said, clasping her hands. "I'm proud to be her husband."

"You'll treat her as good as she deserves?"

"No," Brandt said with a shake of his head. "I'll treat her better, because I'm still not sure that I deserve her." She seemed pleased by his answer, and they exchanged cheek kisses before she returned to her seat. Rawlings drew alongside him, playfully punching him on the arm.

"Damned tie," he said, "choking me. You owe for me this, Conner."

"I set up the first date between you and your fiancée," Brandt reminded him. "Didn't I?"

"Crap," Rawlings answered, then laughed hoarsely. "She looks good, doesn't she?" he said, motioning toward Rowan. She met his eyes, and shot him a come-hither look. "I'm a lucky man."

Brandt held up his drink, toasting Rawlings. "We both are, bud—we both are."

"Amen."

"What are you two grinning about?" Mitchell asked amiably. "As if I didn't already know."

"I was just giving Brandt some tips for his wedding night, Mitch," Rawlings joked.

"I wouldn't worry too much about that," Mitchell said. "It looks like he's already put a smile on his wife's face." They glanced toward Marissa, who was trying to maintain a conversation with every single woman at once. She looked harried, but also drop-dead beautiful and as happy as any woman ever had. Brandt lifted his glass in silent toast to her, and she smiled back at him. God, that smile—the place where it'd all started, along with a roll of fence wire and a few tomato plants. But the smile, and the love that came from it, was the thing that mattered most on that day.

• • •

"You absolutely have to come to our wedding," Rowan implored Josie. "I need you as a bridesmaid."

"Really?" she asked. "That's so kind of you. Will there be men there?"

Rowan laughed. "I have two brothers and a cousin who will fight for the honor of escorting you down the aisle."

"You twisted my arm," Josie said, smiling. "We'll go dress shopping soon."

"Sounds good." She sighed. "Marissa? Has the bride gone into a wedding-induced stupor?"

Marissa turned her attention back toward them and smiled. "Sorry, I was just looking at Brandt in his suit. My man cleans up pretty good."

"So does mine," Rowan said. "I'm thinking I'd like to get him alone, wearing nothing but that tie…"

"Take it easy," Marissa said, stifling a laugh. "Here comes my mom." The younger women continued to chat amongst themselves as Connie carefully hugged her daughter, taking extra care not to mess up her dress.

"I'm not sure any child of mine has a right to look so beautiful," she said apologetically, "but you do. It's no wonder Brandt couldn't take his eyes off you during the ceremony."

Marissa smiled, a cursory glance across the room confirming her suspicions. "He still can't."

"A word of advice?" Connie offered. Marissa nodded. "Let him have the upper hand once in a while. Keep that smile on his face."

Marissa laughed and kissed her mother on the cheek. "Thank you, Mom. Thank you for everything."

"You're welcome, sweetie. I'm pretty sure your other mom wants to talk with you for a moment, so I'm headed for the dessert table. Again."

Marissa laughed, and Laura stopped alongside her, watching the surroundings, seemingly gathering up her thoughts. "You remind me of myself on my own wedding day," she said. "Although less nervous."

"It's a good façade on my part," Marissa admitted. "I'm terrified. Not of Brandt, of course, but of not being a good wife."

"That comes with time," Laura replied. "But you both seem to have the basic ingredients in hand: love and understanding."

"We're going to be happy."

"Yes," Laura said, pulling her into a hug. "Of that I am sure."

• • •

Mitchell and Laura did something a little backwards, but much appreciated for the newlyweds: they rented hotel rooms for the guests, leaving Brandt and Marissa the house, and the ranch, all to themselves. After stuffing the guests with food, and taking about a thousand photographs, everyone dispersed, Laura putting away the leftovers before bidding them goodbye for the evening. When they were alone, Brandt carried Marissa up to his room and sighed as he drank in her body, admiring its form and shape even through the layers of white fabric.

"This probably isn't the honeymoon of your dreams," he apologized, tugging his tie loose, his fingers working the knot free.

Marissa turned her back to him so he could unzip her dress. "Is my husband here?" she asked.

Brandt looked around playfully. "He is."

"Then it's the honeymoon of my dreams."

And mine too, he thought, glancing around his childhood bedroom. This moment had been the setting for more than a few fantasies over the years, albeit without the wedding. Knowing he'd spend the rest of his life with this woman somehow made the reality better. He brushed her long, curled strands of golden hair away from her back, placing his lips to her spine as he let down the zipper.

"I changed my mind," she informed him. "My dreams never felt this good."

He stood up, and pushed the dress off her shoulders slowly until it was a heap in the floor. He turned her around, pulling her from the white lace and into his arms. "I'm going to remember this moment for the rest of my life," he said hoarsely. "How beautiful you looked, how much I wanted you." He stopped long enough to remove his suit jacket, every muscle in his body tensing up. Her fingers found the buttons of his shirt, unfastening them slowly, her thumbs slipping in the opening and stroking his chest. He couldn't take much more of this—how could he want her this much, when they'd just made love the previous night? Simple—it was their honeymoon, and if you were lucky, you only had one— or maybe a lifetime of them.

His shirt fell to the floor, and seconds later he'd pinned her to the bed. He kissed his way along her neck and chest, heard her breath catching in her throat. She helped him out of his trousers and underwear—neither of which was easy—and he did the same for her, barely able to contain himself. He entered with a deep thrust, felt her warmth envelop him as she arched into his stomach and hips. He wanted to prolong the moment, but his movements were too rapid, and her need was too great.

"Brandt," she said dreamily, her voice wonderfully detached.

"What, sweetheart?" he whispered in her ear, his breath coming quicker now.

"Promise me it'll always be like this."

He laughed, and as he did, he felt his muscles loosen. "It will," he said, pulling her hips toward him as the first climax unspooled. "It will, beautiful."

• • •

Marissa collapsed atop Brandt's chest with a contented sigh. Every inch of their bodies was drenched in sweat, and a faint sense of exhaustion was creeping into her bones.

"I don't think this is normal," she told him. He laughed through closed lips.

"I don't think it's normal, either," Brandt replied, "but it sure as hell feels good." His knuckles massaged her back, running up and down either side of her spine. If he was tired, he wasn't letting it show. He looked sated, and maybe a tad arrogant, but she figured he'd earned the right. They'd been making love for what felt like hours, barely taking a moment to catch their breath before going at it again. There hadn't been much in the way of pillow talk, either, which was fine—they'd have the rest of their lives to talk.

Before she had time to react, he'd rolled her onto her back once again. "I think I'm tired," she lied. "I think I need to sleep."

He looked down at her and grinned. "You're a horrible liar," he joked, "but good at everything else."

His hand drifted downward, across her stomach. "Just 'good'?" she asked, feigning hurt.

He laughed again. "I don't remember you being this cocky before."

"Men are cocky," she reminded him. "Women are self-assured." His hand slid between her thighs. His fingers slipped inside, his palm resting against her, pressing hard, then making small circles. When his mouth moved lower, tugging against her breasts until his breath hitched in his throat, she thought the fire would consume her and destroy what little sense of reason she left.

He pushed her thighs apart and entered her, hot and solid, and she rose to meet him. His mouth met hers again, her tongue teasing and tantalizing his until he was groaning deep in his chest. "Stop," he said weakly, laughter edging against the word. "You're killing me." She pulled him downward into her, found no resistance on his part as she began to unspool, wracking and twisting into him as the waves moved through her body. It was enough to drag him over the edge, and he covered her mouth with his as he came, silencing the hoarse gasp that had built in his chest. She held him tightly as the aftershocks continued, his release filling her until he stilled in her embrace. She reached up to brush the hair away from his face, and rubbed her lips across his until he was fully involved, his mouth hot and ardent.

"Damn," he said roughly as he floated back to earth. "I thought you said you were tired?"

"You called me a liar," she kidded.

Her hand stroked his hip, then the base of his stomach and finally points further south. He pulsed inside her, clearly not out of the game yet. "I'll never do that again," he swore. "You look beautiful, by the way."

Her other hand was at the nape of his neck, trailing through the fine hair at the back of his head. "Thank you. And, Brandt?"

"Yeah?" he asked, smiling like a fool.

"I enjoy the teasing. It may be the best part."

He nearly withdrew from her hips, before sliding to the depths of her yet again. "I thought this was the best part?"

She laughed, tugging him down until there wasn't a whit of space between their bodies. "I lied again." And when he lowered his mouth onto hers, a smile crinkling the corners of his eyes, she didn't mind at all being silenced.

• • •

Brandt awoke somewhere around dawn, dragged on a pair of jeans, and went downstairs to brew a pot of coffee. When he returned with a large, steaming cup, he found Marissa asleep under his blanket, her hair splayed across the pillow, as golden as a field of wheat. He smiled, turned toward the window, and smiled again. Then he heard a stirring, and footsteps as Marissa, clad only in his white dress shirt, pressed herself to his back and looped her arms beneath his, finally crossing them over his chest.

"Good morning, Mrs. Conner."

Her face rested against his shoulder. "Good morning, Mr. Conner."

"I didn't mean to wake you," he apologized.

"You didn't," she said. Their voices were sleep-roughened. "The coffee woke me."

He handed her his cup and smiled. "It's strong," he warned her.

She took a sip and hugged him a little tighter. "Just the way I like it."

The sun was rising through his east-facing window, breaking across the horizon with orange streaks, shattering the night sky until it turned a brilliant shade of cobalt.

"This makes me not want to move to the city," she said, exhaling deeply.

He twined their fingers together, resting them atop his bare chest, near his heart. "The sunrise?" he mused.

"All of it," she said. "The sunrise, the ranch, waking up in your room…"

He glanced back at her over his shoulder. "And all the things that put that smile on your face." That beautiful, wondrous smile, and those blue eyes that would make the morning sky jealous. He'd give his last nickel to wake up to that every morning for the rest of his life—but then that voice in the back of his mind let him know that he would, excepting a necessary separation.

She handed him the coffee cup and he finished it. "Could you…you know?"

His eyebrows lifted, and he set down the cup on the windowsill before he turned into her arms. "Again?" She nodded. "Let me figure out a way to get turned on again." He looked from the bottom of her chin, across her mouth and nose, and those brilliant eyes, and up to her forehead. "Okay," he said. "I'm ready."

She laughed softly, the sound music to his ears. "That was it? My face did it?"

His thumbs slid beneath her chin, lifting her mouth up toward his. "Every time," he replied, shaking his head. "Every time."

Epilogue

Two Years Later

There was a rap against the doorframe, and Marissa looked up from her desk to see Rowan's smiling face. "Ready to head home, Madame Guidance Counselor?"

Marissa laughed. "More than ready, Mrs. McCoy."

"Did you survive your first week?"

"Without a scratch."

"Good, good. I'm heading out now. I want to pick up little Mitch before I go home. Laura's a real trooper, babysitting that kid with no complaints. I know he's a handful. Hell, he's half-mine."

Marissa laughed again. "Nonsense. He's adorable. Anyway, I still have a few things to take care of here. See you at home?"

Rowan nodded. "I'll see you there."

When she was alone, Marissa looked around the office and smiled to herself. This job was the culmination of two difficult years of work—studying, exams, assistantships, internships, sleepless nights, and too damned much time away from her husband.

Her husband. Marissa still had to pinch herself at times, primarily when she woke up and saw Brandt's handsome face on the other pillow. She wondered if Brandt knew that he smiled in his sleep, that he sometimes pulled her close and whispered "I love you" without ever opening his eyes. It was instinctual, the way he loved her, the way he held her tight and caressed her. How many men, she thought, could have so unselfishly pushed the woman they loved into pursuing her dreams when it meant a lot of lonely nights? They'd more than made up for it during Christmas breaks, and long weekends, and the entire summer following her graduation. If Brandt ever grew tired, he didn't let it show—his desire for her, the love she felt when they were together, was astounding and impossible for her to put into words.

Following their honeymoon, Brandt had moved her into a clean apartment near campus, and helped unpack and set up everything from cable to grocery delivery. He'd inspected the place top-to-bottom until he was sure there were no problems, and made sure they broke in her new bed before he reluctantly drove home all by himself. They talked on the phone daily, no matter how busy things got, and he spent weekends and even full weeks with her here and there, cleaning her apartment and cooking her meals while she was hard at work with her classes. Winter was the absolute worst, the loneliest time of the year, when snowstorms kept them far apart and housebound. Brandt still had his cattle, but Marissa knew they were little consolation.

Not long after Brandt and Marissa's own wedding, Rawlings and Rowan were married in a large church in Tennessee, with all of their families in attendance. With Rawlings's father recovered, they moved to the ranch, where Rowan immediately set forth with a major redecorating of the entire bunkhouse—out went his mismatched bachelor pad furniture to Goodwill, and in came the things from her apartment. He only grumbled briefly, because they soon decided to expand their family. Little Mitch came along a year later, a beautiful dark-haired boy named after the man who loved Rawlings like his own son. There was some solace in the fact that they'd been there to keep Brandt company on his loneliest days—the kid affectionately called him "Uncle Bran" even though he could barely speak.

Marissa filed her papers, grabbed her purse, and locked her office. She loved her job, but it was time to head home.

• • •

Brandt elbowed his best friend playfully. "I think you've put on a few pounds, McCoy," he teased.

"I call bullshit," Rawlings shot back, feigning offense. "That's extra muscle. I pack Rowan to bed every night after I massage her feet."

"There goes my appetite," Brandt joked. "I'll never eat again."

"Ha-ha, buddy boy. You mean to tell me you've never given Marissa a massage? Ever?"

Both men were leaned against a fence rail, their eyes cast toward the horizon. The herd of cattle was moving out of sight, no doubt looking for the shade of a copse of trees. This was always the hottest part of summer. In his mind he returned to last night, when he'd massaged Marissa from head to toe—or maybe the other way around—but he wasn't about to tell Rawlings that. "Afraid I don't have the same knack for romance that you do, pal," he said.

Rawlings laughed. "Hmm, sounds like a fib if I ever heard one. Anyway, I'm glad we're all back together again. Now Rowan has someone to share her woman stuff with." Brandt chuckled, then smiled at his friend.

"It hasn't sucked, has it? Being married?"

"It's been the best thing that ever happened to me," Rawlings said thoughtfully.

"Me too," Brandt replied. "Me too." Car wheels made a noise behind them as Rowan pulled to a stop.

"There's my woman," Rawlings said, a huge grin on his face, "and my boy."

Brandt nodded. "You're not getting too crowded in the bunkhouse, are you?"

Rawlings shrugged. "It's a little tight, but we can't complain. It's big enough for a small family."

"We'll talk to Dad about adding on next year," Brandt promised. "I'm pretty sure he'll buy the lumber."

"I like the sound of that," he told Brandt. "Later," he said, and Brandt nodded goodbye to him. He smiled as he took in the scene of domestic happiness: Rawlings giving Rowan a welcome-home kiss, and pulling the small boy from his car seat and into his big arms. The toddler laughed, the joyous sounds echoing into the yard long after they'd disappeared into the bunkhouse.

He'd have that soon, he knew, and that made him smile again.

A good portion of the previous two years had been spent putting together the log cabin where Mitchell and Laura now resided. It was situated between the old house and the roadway, and hidden so well by the trees that it was barely even visible in winter. Laura was thrilled with having a small space to clean, and Mitchell still helped with the ranch on a daily basis. Otherwise they didn't bother their son too much—they could see the happiness apparent on his face each and every day, and that was satisfaction enough for them. They spent most of their time together on Sundays, during and after church, when Laura helped Marissa in the kitchen as she prepped a huge meal for the seven of them.

Soon to be eight.

Brandt attended church every Sunday now that Marissa was home. He had a lot to be thankful for, and putting on his good suit was always a nice reminder of the best day of his life—the day Marissa became his wife.

He was on the porch now, ready to head inside, when her car pulled to a stop. Marissa stepped outside and practically ran into his arms. He received her gratefully. God, she was perfect.

"You act like you missed me today," he observed. "For the record, I missed you too."

She hugged him, her head bent down against his chest. "I love you, Brandt. I just hope we made the right decision."

His hand rested over her abdomen, the place where a new life was growing. It sent a powerful sense of both pride and deep, abiding love through his veins. His protective instincts were kicking in. "Did you tell anyone yet?"

"Only my mother." She sighed, then looked up into his eyes. She was vulnerable, but the furthest thing from fragile he could imagine. She was steadfast, tough as a piece of iron. She was all his. "Do you think we chose the wrong time to have a baby? I just started my job."

His hand continued to stroke her belly. "There's never a wrong time to have a baby when you're this much in love," he reminded her. "Besides, I can't wait to meet Brandt Junior."

She gave him a look of admiration. "Brandt, Jr.? How do you know it's a boy?"

He smiled, readying his lips to meet hers. "I just know, beautiful," he said softly. "I just know."

A Sneak Peek from Crimson Romance
(From *The Bargain* by Christine S. Feldman)

It was like living in the story of Beauty and the Beast, Shannon decided, something many women probably would think had great potential for romance and happy-ever-after love. Too bad she was cast in the role of the beast.

Sitting cross-legged on the faded floral quilt her grandmother made many years ago, Shannon turned another well-worn page in her high school yearbook and took a cautious sip of her morning coffee, wincing at the heat of it and then blowing on the rest in an effort to spare her mouth from third-degree burns. Somewhere downstairs in her living room was an invitation for her ten-year high school reunion that had recently come in the mail. Its arrival brought a lot of memories to mind, most of which she would rather forget, but there were a few highlights that had driven her to dig out her old yearbooks. The one on her lap was from her senior year.

There weren't very many pictures of her in this particular book beyond the requisite senior picture, which was probably not such a bad thing. She frowned down at the image taken nearly ten years ago. The smile was tight-lipped, hiding the braces from the unforgiving camera.

Ah, well. At least in black and white it wasn't so obvious that her hair looked like an exploding fireball of color. She wasn't interested in her own picture anyway.

Turning the page quickly, she found the face she wanted.

Andrew Kingston.

She traced her fingers over his features. He went by Drew now. Either way suited him, but he thought Drew made him more approachable to his constituents somehow, more boy-next-door.

Maybe he was right. What did she really know about politics anyway?

Drew had been class president. Politics was in his blood, and he was good at it, too. The kind of politician who would get things done and keep his promises. She brought the cup to her mouth for another sip of coffee as she contemplated his classically handsome features. And who knew, maybe one day—"Ow!"

Coffee was still too hot. Shannon fanned her open mouth and said a bad word.

Her shaggy mongrel, Bo, cocked an ear at her and gave her a disapproving look.

"Well, it's hot!"

He gave her another look as if to say *duh* before yawning hugely and rolling over on the bed to allow her better access to his belly.

"Subtle," Shannon said, but she obliged him and scratched his stomach with one hand while turning her attention back to Drew's picture. She didn't know why she tortured herself like this. He barely noticed her then, and he barely noticed her now. About the only thing that had changed was now her teeth were straighter, thanks to the hateful braces.

She flipped a few pages back to a place she had turned to so many times before that the pages naturally fell open to it now. A candid picture, students lolling around a grassy knoll of picnic tables at lunchtime, arms around each other's shoulders in a pose for the camera. And right in the center? Drew, of course. Close-cropped hair, broad shoulders, and an even broader grin. A couple of girls on either side smiled adoringly at him instead of at the camera.

There were lots of pictures with Drew in them. And in every picture, he was surrounded by friends—and usually girls. There were plenty of girls carrying a torch for him in high school, and Shannon had been one of them.

"Still am," she murmured ruefully, closing the yearbook. It would have been so much easier to get over him and move on if he were a jerk, but unfortunately he was not. He was kind, intelligent, and as handsome as ever. And so she was basically screwed, because in ten years, give or take, he had never seen her as anything more than "good old Shannon," and it was doubtful he ever would. She could probably show up to work naked, and he would still hand her papers to file without so much as batting an eye. For a moment Shannon let herself indulge in a fantasy in which she showed up to Drew's office wearing something red, revealing, and *highly* inappropriate for work. A smile played on her lips.

Then she glanced at the clock on her nightstand and scrambled off the bed to pull a pair of sensible slacks out from her closet.

Minutes later, she sprinted down the stairs with coffee cup in hand, neatly sidestepping an assortment of tools she neglected to put away last night before dragging her tired body to bed. No matter. She'd need them again tonight to finish the tiling in the kitchen, so really she was just saving herself time this way.

Shannon finished the coffee, fed Bo, and pulled her hair back into its usual braid without needing to look in the mirror to check her handiwork. Grabbing a stack of folders and a breakfast bar, she swung her purse over her shoulder and hurried out the front door.

It was coming along despite what the naysayers told her in the beginning, she thought with some satisfaction as she paused by the side of her truck long enough to give the old house a quick appraisal. Most of the work she had done on the place so far was on the inside to make it more habitable, but the porch was no longer falling apart and the crumbling front steps were no longer a safety hazard. She was better with tools than she was with plants, but maybe she would venture to add a couple baskets of flowers for some color.

It was nothing fancy, but it was hers.

And it was secluded, she thought, starting up the engine and pulling out of the long, graveled driveway. Peaceful. Granted, the extra minutes it took to drive back inside the city limits were a pain—especially when she was on the verge of running late like today—but she loved the quiet solitude that surrounded her place.

Her place. She still had trouble believing it sometimes. Shannon Mahoney, homeowner. Sure, Drew Kingston was still virtually oblivious to her as a woman, but she had come a long way since high school. Now if only she could get him to see it.

Spring weather was turning nicely into summer, and the drive into the city was pleasant. Or it would have been if she took the time to notice it. Her speedometer edged past the posted speed limit when she glanced at her watch, and she forced herself to slow down. Better late than ticketed for speeding, she reminded herself through gritted teeth. With the money she poured into the house lately, she could barely afford gas let alone a ticket. Still, it was with great relief that she turned into the parking lot and saw Drew's sedan was not yet in its spot. Right, she told herself with an inward eye roll, because men are so turned on by punctuality.

Oh, well.

She had not, however, beaten Clarissa into work. The woman was twice Shannon's age and still perky enough for both of them. "Morning, Shan!" she said with a cheery wave as she glanced up from her desk in the main office.

"Morning."

The older blonde gave Shannon a once-over and clucked disapprovingly. "Beige, beige, and more beige. Don't you own anything else, honey?"

"Sure. Tan."

"Not funny. There's a nice figure lurking somewhere under those boring old clothes of yours. You only get to be young once, Shannon. You ought to be making the most of it."

"I'm doing just fine."

Clarissa raised one eyebrow. "Are you sure?"

She thought her cheeks might be turning pink, not a good color combination with her hair. "You know what? I think I hear Drew's phone ringing."

"Liar."

Shrugging unapologetically, Shannon beat a hasty retreat and unlocked the door that led to her desk and to Drew's office. It was only a temporary reprieve, she knew. Clarissa's youngest child had gone off to college last fall, and apparently she thought Shannon was as good a means as any to combat empty nest syndrome. It did no good to remind her that Shannon already had parents, thank you very much. They were off enjoying what they liked to call early retirement in Florida—it sounded better than "sitting around unemployed"—and Clarissa clearly felt that such long-distance parenting didn't count. She might be right.

Shannon flipped the lights on and dropped her armload of files on her desk, careful not to let any of their papers spill out. There was a week's worth of work invested in the top one alone, and time was too scarce around here to risk having to redo any of it unnecessarily. Not that she minded the work. She began humming under her breath as she opened the door to Drew's small office and positioned the window blinds to let in the morning sun the way she knew he liked it. She was good at organizing things and being efficient, and she appreciated the steady paycheck. Winding up as assistant to councilman Drew Kingston had been an unexpected bonus.

Bonus? Delight would be a better word.

Drew had not actually been the one to hire her; that honor went to his predecessor. The day newly elected Drew Kingston walked through the door in his perfect suit and matching tie, Shannon decided maybe, just maybe, miracles did occasionally happen to ordinary folks like her.

Sunlight splayed through the blinds and landed on a thin sheaf of official papers on Drew's desktop. She glanced at them in passing. The youth center. Shannon knew those papers backward and forward by now. Drew probably did, too. Was he having second thoughts? She pictured him sitting alone in his office the night before, reviewing everything and wondering if he was really ready to do this. It was his brainchild, but maybe the cost was too personal not to reconsider it at least a little bit. He might be her dream man, but he was still only human, after all.

Returning to her own desk, Shannon tore open the wrapper of her breakfast bar as she glanced at the clock. Budget meeting at ten o'clock, she thought as she took a bite and then opened up the calendar on her computer. The upcoming charity auction… Then there was that zoning issue for him to look at before next Thursday. Anticipating his request, she had already begun to delve into that for him.

The phone rang, interrupting her train of thought. She choked down the bite of dried fruit and granola mixture, trying not to make a face. She really ought to start eating a real breakfast. "Drew Kingston's office," she said with a voice raspy from granola that hadn't quite made it down her throat yet. "How may I help—"

"I want to talk to Drew. Now."

Great, she thought sourly. One of those. Nothing like beginning the day with a surly citizen. "Mr. Kingston is not available at the moment. I could take a message, if you like."

There was a humorless laugh on the other end. "Right. What is that, code for 'he's screening calls'?"

"It means he's not available." Her tone was cool. Even a city councilman got his share of angry callers, and Shannon had no qualms about keeping them at bay.

"Bull. He's hiding in his office, isn't he?"

Her voice got even cooler. "Mr. Kingston *doesn't* hide."

"No? Because it seems like he went out of his way to keep a low profile on this one, sweetheart."

What was this loon talking about?

Forget it. She heard the front door open then and Clarissa greet Drew. He didn't need to start his day out on a sour note like this. "I'm sorry, sir. Mr. Kingston naturally wants to listen to the concerns of constituents, and he values their feedback, but he's very busy at this time. Why don't you call back later and schedule an appointment? Have a very nice day."

"Don't you dare hang—"

She let the phone fall back on the receiver, feeling just a little bit wicked and not the least bit sorry.

"Good morning, Shannon."

As it always did when she saw Drew, her heart tightened a little inside her chest. "Good morning."

Trim and polished, he was what every politician wished they looked like. The suit was expensive but worth every penny since it fit him so well. His shoulders were just as broad as they had been in high school and his body just as lean. Nowadays he had an air of maturity about him that he hadn't quite earned back then, but his smile was still boyish in its charm. "Everything all set for the budget meeting?"

She nodded and held out a file for him.

"Wonderful," he said, looking through it. "Eleven o'clock?"

"Ten."

"Oh, that's right. Thanks. What would I do without you?" Drew smiled again, but it was with less energy than usual.

For the first time, Shannon noticed dark circles under his eyes. "You look tired. Can I get you anything? Some coffee?"

"No, thanks. I've had four cups already. Any more caffeine and I'll be too jittery to hold my pen steady."

She hesitated, wanting to ask if everything was all right but not sure if her asking would make him think she was being too presumptuous somehow. Then he disappeared into his office and closed the door behind him, and the moment was gone.

Coward, she thought to herself.

A short while later she knocked cautiously on his door to deliver a piece of mail to him.

"Come in."

She opened the door to see him seated behind his desk and staring out the window. "Sorry," she said. "This was just messengered over, though, so…"

He nodded toward his desk, and she let the letter fall onto it. Then he went back to staring out the window.

Just say it, she told herself. *Ask* him already. "Is everything all right?" she blurted out finally.

There. She had said it, and miracle of miracles, he didn't look shocked or offended. Was basic conversation this hard for everyone, she wondered, or just for her?

"Oh, sure," he said with a slight sigh and a shrug of his shoulders. "It's just…Do you have any family, Shannon?"

"Me?" she asked, surprised. "I…well, parents. A couple of cousins maybe that I haven't seen in years."

"Parents still living?"

She knew his were not. "Yes."

"That's nice," he said faintly. "No brothers or sisters, though."

"No."

"Mmm," was all he said, and he went back to staring out the window.

Now what? she wondered. Ask him again? Turn around and leave? She froze like a wild animal caught in the headlights of an oncoming car. How could any woman be this inept around a man?

Drew saved her by speaking again. "This youth center…"

"Yes?" she said hopefully.

He turned to look at her and frowned. "Do you think…" He trailed off, his fingers rifling idly through the papers she had spotted earlier on his desk.

"Yes?" she repeated.

But he seemed to think better of whatever he was going to say. "Never mind. I shouldn't be keeping you from your work like this. Don't mind me."

Feeling a little disappointed, Shannon turned to go.

"Oh, Shannon?"

She turned back, hope sparking anew. Would he confide in her after all? Thank her for her concern? Be touched that she cared enough to ask after him?

"Could you do me a favor?"

"Of course. What is it?" *Comfort you? Hold your hand? Have your baby, maybe?*

Drew looked a little sheepish. "I have a dinner date tonight, but I forgot to make reservations. Could you call Le Joli and ask for a table for two? Seven o'clock. Something with a view, preferably."

A pang shot through her, but Shannon kept her expression carefully neutral. "Sure. Anything else?"

"No, that's it, thanks. Good old Shannon. You're a lifesaver." And he treated her to one more charming smile as she closed the door behind her on her way out.

Good old Shannon.

Pulling up the restaurant's number on her computer as she sat down, Shannon wrote herself a note to call them when they opened for lunch. There was nothing surprising about Drew's request. She had done the same thing for him many times before. It just hurt a little more each time she did it.

Good old Shannon wouldn't fit in at a fine French restaurant, she thought with a glance down at her clothes and a slight hitch in her throat. She cleared it quickly. Good old Shannon was not the type of girl a man thought of when he thought of a romantic dinner for two. Good old Shannon wasn't really the type of girl a man thought about at all.

Maybe with the right clothes, a little makeup …

Her mother's voice popped into her head, her words an echo from some childhood memory. *You can put a pig in satin and pearls, baby, but it won't change the fact that a pig is still a pig.*

Now where had that come from? she wondered, frowning as she struggled to remember. Her mother had never been insensitive enough to actually imply Shannon bore any kind of resemblance to a pig. Her memory cleared. No, it was back in high school when Shannon had started talking about maybe going to college after all. Her bewildered parents hadn't seen much point to it. They certainly hadn't understood why she bothered to put herself through night school. Come to think of it, there were a lot of things they didn't understand.

Which could be one reason why she didn't call Florida very often.

But for just a moment, sitting there, aching over Drew's obliviousness to her, Shannon found herself wishing her mother were a little closer than Florida. Well, she would wish that if her mother were a little more like June Cleaver and a little less like Peg Bundy—or at least a little more like Clarissa.

"Clarissa?" she called out through her open door.

"Yes?" the other woman's voice floated back to her.

"Want to adopt me?"

"Sure thing, honey."

Shannon smiled faintly and forced her attention away from Drew and onto her work. This was hardly a productive line of thinking. Time to get back to zoning issues.

She made very little headway amid phone calls and emails that kept interrupting her, but she did her best to shut out both the distraction in her heart and the chatter between Clarissa and the occasional visitor. Her eyes were glued to her computer screen, so she couldn't help but let out a startled gasp when a pair of large masculine hands came down on her desktop, one on either side of her computer.

She looked up to see just who had invaded her personal space so abruptly.

"Hello," said a dark-haired, dark-eyed personification of sin. "Remember me? I believe you hung up on me earlier."

About the Author

Tommie Conrad lives in rural Appalachia and holds degrees from the University of Kentucky in both Psychology and Library and Information Science. You can follow Tommie's writing at *http://tommieconrad.blogspot.com*.

In the mood for more Crimson Romance?
Check out *Crashing the Congressman's Wedding*
by Elley Arden
at *CrimsonRomance.com*.

www.ingramcontent.com/pod-product-compliance
Lightning Source LLC
Chambersburg PA
CBHW010302100726
47904CB00011B/2716